Some Other Books by David R. Slavitt

GET THEE TO A NUNNERY

A Pair of Shakespearean Divertimentos

by David R. Slavitt

CATBIRD PRESS

CATBIRD PRESS
16 Windsor Road, North Haven, CT 06473
800-360-2391; catbird@pipeline.com
www.catbirdpress.com

Our books are distributed by
Independent Publishers Group

Library of Congress Cataloging-in-Publication

Slavitt, David R., 1935-
[Lorenzo's book]
Get thee to a nunnery : a pair of Shakespearean divertimentos
/ by David R. Slavitt.
Contents: Lorenzo's book -- Luke's book.
1. Shakespeare, William, 1564-1616--Adaptations.
I. Shakespeare, William, 1564-1616. Romeo and Juliet.
II. Shakespeare, William, 1564-1616. Measure for Measure.
III. Slavitt, David R., 1935- . Luke's book. IV. Title.
PR2878.R6S54 1999
813'.54--dc21   98-45088 CIP

Contents

O the rare tricks of a Machivillian!
He doth not come like a gross plodding slave
And buffet you to death. No, my quaint knave,
He tickles you to death; makes you die laughing;
As if you had swallow'd down a pound of saffron.

—John Webster, *The White Devil* V, iii, 195-199

Luke's Book

I

THE QUESTION BEFORE US — and, let's not kid ourselves, it is always before us — is, what do we mean by civilization? The grand buildings of Europe, the palaces, churches, and universities full of paintings, sculptures, and books, ringing with the echoes of great music and witty talk . . . Is that it? Is that even real? Or, more to the point, does it oblige the rest of us to aspire, and of course to fail, as we try to imitate those princes whose great-grandfathers were brigands, pirates, thugs, and butchers, just like ours but more successful because they were better at it?

Simplify, simplify. What you are left with is that clearer statement of the problem the cowboy or prospector sees as he comes riding or maybe crawling into town. What is he looking for after his strenuous months in the wilderness? A bath, a drink, a decent meal cooked on an actual stove, some nookie maybe, and then, at the end of his brief binge, some fresh supplies and new equipment so that he can go out to seek, once again, his fortune from the flesh of dumb beasts or the hidden veins of metal God or the Devil hid in those hillsides, barren and absurdly remote.

Civilization, for him, is the huddle of shacks near a bend in the river: a barber shop, a saloon, a general store, and a

whore house. The town, an outpost of what we cannot deny
is the zero grade of society and, indeed, of civilized living.
Some of these towns are better than others, of course. In a
few of them the liquor is even drinkable, the food edible; the
prices are not outrageous and the odds are a little longer
against getting robbed (with a deck of cards or a naked six-
shooter) or coming down with the clap. That would be a good
town, but there aren't a lot of those. Most are bad, and some
are worse.

And the worst? Wurst, which is why they called it that,
at least at first. The Wurst town you ever did see. After a
while, when that joke wore thin, the name changed or, say if
you prefer, evolved to Hotdog, which was the same old Wurst
with a little relish and mustard. And I suppose Vienna is what
they'll claim to be one day — or, maybe, Frankfurt — out
there in the New Mexico scrub that looks nothing whatever
like the Vienna woods.

How do you think people decide to settle in a place like
Hotdog anyway, this huddle of weatherworn buildings with
a joke name and a bad reputation? These are not successful,
reputable citizens from back East who have come out for the
pretty sunsets and the fresh air. These are failures and fugitives, the world's washouts who have, like dirty water, sunk
with unseemly gurgles of complaint to find at last their proper
level. Despised and disenchanted, they come out here mostly
to get away from something. Sometimes they come in the
hope of finding something. Some of them have vague notions
of striking it rich, but this is a pro forma dream in which not
even the devoutly stupid really believe. It is a logical possibility perhaps, but in their sober moments they know it's not
going to happen, and that if it does, they'll get robbed or
cheated, and either killed outright or, worse, left to dispose of

themselves, with guilt, shame, disgust, and despair in whatever combination these have oozed up from the spirit's wound.

They also come to such places just to die, having been told that a bullet is a faster and cleaner death than what consumption is likely to offer. They come to the crest of the pass, look down at this child's toy of a town, this pathetic collection of unlovely structures, and recognize it as their fated place. Its ugliness is what speaks to them, its unadorned meanness familiar, right, and true. A man can all but hear his own name in the wind's moan and take it as the raspy voice of the avenging angel who has been following him as long as he can remember, hounding him even to this dismal hidey-hole at the end of the world.

Him? Me, I might better say. I'm Lucas Wright. Or was once. Out here it's just Luke. The surname is a cruel homonym, a bad joke I haven't bothered with for a long time. I can still remember clearly how, as I descended from the pass to the town below and approached the ramshackle rectangles of the buildings on its single street, I felt the special satisfaction that comes of fitting an odd-shaped puzzle piece into its proper place. Here in this minimalist assertion of mankind's claim to be a social species, I figured I had at last found a place in which I was unlikely to be disillusioned or disappointed. The pretensions by which most men think their lives are demonstrations of ethics, esthetics, morality, and religion were too delicate to flourish here. In the shadows of board rooms and boudoirs, hypocrisy can all too easily beguile the gullible, but in the glare of this unrelieved sunlight, even a fool like me would be unable to mistake the harsh truths of the human condition.

Say that your wife has run off with another man, taking your daughter with her, and say too that your wife's lover's wealth and power are such that you have no possible recourse and, indeed, are forced to agree with his lawyer, whose manicure is too perfect and who smells too strongly of rosewater, that by any reasonable standard your daughter is better off with the advantages money can buy. What choice is there but to give up the foolish notions you once had of love, trust, and truth, and accede to the suggestion that you just disappear? Clear out of town? It isn't that you'd be doing your wife a favor, or even yourself, but you'd be doing what's best for your little girl.

Go west. That's what the West is for, isn't it? Those who don't fit anymore, who are an inconvenience to others or to themselves, can go there, vanish the way the sun does when it dips down below the horizon. And not bother anyone with meaningless reproaches and useless recriminations — not to speak of the empty, ludicrous threats — which are anyway likely to get you hurt or killed if they continue . . . ("Do I make myself quite clear, Mr. Wright?")

Not that I'm admitting anything exactly like that ever happened to me. But one way or another, most of us out here in Hotdog have come because we had to and stayed because it suits us. We may not delight in it, but it fits — like a beat-up old hat that sits the right way on the head, so that after a while it's hard to say where the face ends and the hat's droopy, weather-stained brim begins.

What gave that dreary collection of shacks and sheds its special quality of strenuous despair was the vista of sky overhead, a rich and altogether pointless display of irrelevant splendor that would have been impressive and intimidating above any ordinary human settlement. Here that huge expanse of pale blue with its random displays of towering clouds turned the town into a joke, a contemptible blemish on the bare and all but overwhelming landscape.

As I approached it that first time, I wondered whether it wasn't a ghost town. But no, there was laundry flapping on a clothesline out behind one of the buildings. And there were delicate wisps of smoke here and there. But nobody was moving. They were all inside . . . by coincidence? Or was there a plague? Or were they all fugitives, looking to see if their visitor might be some kind of lawman?

In a town like this, any stranger is a threat. But this is always true, isn't it? That was the whole point of the old Greek notion of hospitality — which is crazy. You may or may not like your neighbors, and may not trust them very far, but you have learned what they're likely to do. And with a stake in the place, they have as much to lose as you do. But any wandering lunatic or desperado can come in from the desert to shoot the town up for reasons that have nothing to do with you, or for no reason at all. Looking out from behind their walls and sighting down the barrels of their rifles, the populace of Hotdog watched as I came toward them, eyeing me with various mixtures of anticipation, greed, and apprehension. I was apprehensive too, I guess, because I had been on the trail a long time and was tired, hoping at least to rest up here for a day or two.

One way of judging a town is by its sheriff. If they've got themselves a drunk, or maybe some bad-ass they've thought to tame down by giving him a badge and a key to the jail house he's already familiar with, then you've got yourself a rough town. After a while, places like that either settle down to something more or less recognizable and hold an election, with a sheriff, a mayor, and a judge to share the power and keep tabs on one another, or else the town just disintegrates, abandoning the pretense of that tin star, which nobody actually needs in order to operate a revolver.

Usually, this test works well enough, but with the Duke it was still an open question. He hadn't yet decided the answer, himself. Duke wasn't necessarily his name, although it could have been Something Duke, or even Duke Something. Personal questions weren't safe to ask in Hotdog. But people called him the Duke, and he was the proprietor of the Black Garter, which was the town's bar, restaurant, hotel, and casino. I assume he also had some interest in Marianne's place down the street, which was the whore house. His managerial duties included maintaining some degree of order and decorum, if only to protect his liquor bottles, his furniture, and his girls from random mayhem. It wasn't unusual for that kind of monitoring to extend beyond the threshold of the premises, to include the rest of the street, which, in this case, meant the whole town. And that was what had happened.

Where the Duke came from and what kind of life he'd had before he hit bottom and arrived at Hotdog, I have no idea. But Claude, one of the layabouts who hung around the Black Garter, dealing a little faro sometimes or just being friendly so that he could cadge drinks and help himself to an occasional pickled egg from the bar, cautioned me early on to watch myself with the Duke. Such a warning was probably gratuitous, as one generally watches oneself with large, mean-looking guys who carry six-guns. But what he had in mind wasn't the Duke's size or meanness or even his ability with a gun, but something far more unpredictable and therefore ominous. "You take care around the Duke," Claude told me in a lazy accent that might have been from the upper south. "He's an intellectual."

And then, in the way of punctuation, he produced a kind of abrupt horse laugh, but it was difficult to say who the butt of his joke was supposed to be — the Duke, me, or Claude himself.

I must have shown my puzzlement. For all I know, that flicker of uncertainty was just what he'd been working toward.

"Buy a drink, stranger?" he asked.

"Sure, why not."

"Hey, Angel! A couple of whiskeys for me and my friend here," he said.

Angel — pronounced in the Spanish way, as On Hell — was the bartender. He was a squat, swarthy fellow with black, beetling eyebrows that formed an uninterrupted line across his forehead, and a livid scar running down his right cheek. He nodded, produced a grudging rictus that I took to be a parody of a smile, and poured us a couple of shots.

He did this slowly and without speaking, and I thought maybe he was an intellectual, too.

*   *   *

Which is not, necessarily, a smart person. Or no smarter than anyone else. An intellectual is somebody who believes in smartness, who thinks it helps, who assumes — for no reason he can ever give — that if you understand a problem well enough, you're halfway to solving it. This is not necessarily true, for if your problem is, by its nature, insoluble, one of the things you're likely to discover about it, after it has been correctly formulated, is that there's no way out. No hope. No prospect of release or even relief. Nothing but the wisdom of dumb beasts to accept that this is how it is.

An intellectual also has a playful side, whether he admits this or not. He is looking to fix things that aren't broken, improve things that can't be improved, and along the way he is always toying with this idea or that. Not only technology and social policy, but morality and religion are entertainments to these people or, even worse, opportunities for self-expression. You and I look around and see a row of buildings, or an expanse of wilderness, and the choice is generally whether to admire it or deplore it, whether to stay for a while or move on. These people, these intellectuals, want to impose their signatures on it.

Even in Hotdog! Or, one might say, especially in Hotdog, which was just that kind of simple community that invites experimentation. After all, what was at risk? This mean-looking collection of shacks might not have been impressive to any sensible man or woman, but to an intellectual it was a micro-environment in which to explore the implications of Rousseau's notions of Social Contract, Aristotle's theories of politics and ethics, or Plato's ideas about the Republic and the philosopher king. It is only on top of the most remote mountains, away from the haze and the blur of cities, that astronomers can see the faintest stars. And here, in Hotdog, in the furthest and most desolate corner of the New Mexico Territory, what we had was, in the poet's phrase, darkness visible.

You'd think that such a place would be hard to fuck up. Even by a nut who seemed to own the town — none of the rest of the citizens found this idea strange in any way — and whose conversational style was, to say the very least, unpredictable.

As a stranger, I got invited to hang around for a spell, if only for the entertainment value novelty promises. The Duke came into town late that afternoon, met me, sized me up, and invited me to dine with him.

I accepted, of course — it would have been rude and perhaps dangerous to refuse. I had the place of honor to the right of the Duke. His boys — associates, cronies, hirelings, enforcers — arranged themselves along the benches that ran down both sides of the trestle table. Cookie brought out a cauldron full of some kind of soup and, in what was evidently a departure from his customary practice, the Duke invited one of his henchmen to say Grace. "Come on, Gaspard. Let's not let our guest think he's fallen among barbarians."

Gaspard, a huge, barrel-chested fellow who was clearly not an intellectual, looked uncomfortable. He grinned like the awkward child he must once have been. "Grace," he said at last, afraid not to play in one of the Duke's games.

"No, no. A real Grace," the Duke said, pretending to be hurt.

Gaspard looked stricken. The joke was apparently going to be on him. He did his best nevertheless: "We thank Thee, O Lord, for this food. Grant us . . . peace on earth."

"That," said the Duke, "was Grace for a barn. For a horse about to stick his nose in his feedbag."

Gaspard stared down at his plate.

Then the Duke laughed heartily, letting him and the rest of us off the hook. "But that's okay, because all horses go to heaven, don't you know!"

"Why is that?" I asked. It had certainly seemed like an invitation for a straight line, and I was the guest, after all.

"In the summer, the sled rests. In the winter, the cart rests. But the horse never rests," the Duke said. "That's why horses go to heaven."

Interesting, perhaps, but it was less compelling than the soup, which turned out to be ambrosial — a delicate broth with a mirepoix of carrots and onions, and a subtle combi-

nation of herbs and spices, the kind of food that only inci-
dentally feeds the belly as it delights the palate and nourishes
the spirit.

"Wonderful soup," I said.

"Ain't it!" the Duke agreed, mock-modest.

"Where does the cook come from?" I asked.

This question met with a deserved ripple of laughter.
"Back east, where everything and everyone comes from," the
Duke said. The cook was a Greek who, as I was informed,
answered to any Greek name — Socrates, Sophocles,
Aeschylus, Alcibiades, Homer . . . Whatever. He had come out
to the New Mexico Territory as a kind of experiment, putting the economists' notions of supply and demand to the test.
In Philadelphia, where there were lots of chefs, sous-chefs, and
marmitons, he was a nobody. Out here, however, where
nobody within a thousand miles knew as much as he did
about the preparation of food, the importance and the rarity
of his skills combined to transform him into an important
personage, a honcho, an aristocrat.

"Were the economists right?" I asked.

The Duke gave me a scornful glance to let me know I'd
committed another bêtise. There was the soup in front of me,
this astonishing marmite with all the evidence my senses or
intellect could provide. What made Hotdog livable, what
redeemed it as if with a shining ray of grace that streaked
down into the murk, was Aeschylus' genius. His pride in his
work and the devoted appreciation of his otherwise rude and
uncultivated clientele made him a pillar of the community.
He didn't just read and execute traditional recipes, although
he could do that quite efficiently when he wanted to
celebrate a birthday or the anniversary of some crucial event
in his life or that of the town. Where he really shone was in

his experiments with the local vegetation. He incorporated odd varieties of plants — peppers, in particular — into his general practice, enriching and extending traditional cuisines. He traveled out to the Indian tribes, the nomads who moved with the game and the pueblo dwellers as well, consulting with their medicine men and the old women of the villages, and he got them to share their secrets.

Who knows whether he was trying to improve the world or just amusing himself? One might have accused him too of being an intellectual, except that he was modest and kept his mouth shut.

It was the taste of that soup that made me decide, at least for a while, to hang around.

Hotdog, I began to suspect, might be an interesting place.

*   *   *

A few days, or a few weeks . . . Time is flexible, particularly if one has nothing to look forward to with eagerness or dread. I found a bare but comfortable enough bunk at Julie's place, which Claude had recommended. It was a boarding house that Julie insisted was not a brothel. It might have been something in how I looked, or it might have been her general rule to make this distinction clear.

She wasn't what you'd call a pretty woman, or even attractive in the usual sense, but she was somehow very sexy. Like one of those primitive figurines, she seemed to have been squooshed down by the sculptor's palm, foreshortened, so that what you got was all tits and ass with hardly any waist between them. She was in her late thirties, maybe, and she wore a severe brown dress that buttoned way up to the neck, which was another way of letting the world know that she was no madame or hooker but only an innkeeper, and that all she was offering was that bed and breakfast the sign in the window promised. Not that she had anything against whores and whoring, except that it was a noisy occupation and its exercise could sometimes get rough.

"I'm here for the long haul," she told me as she showed me the room I could have. It was simple, even bare, but clean. And the bed was tolerable. She stood in the open doorway with her hands folded across that capacious shelf of bosom and explained to me in a perfectly matter-of-fact way, "You want your pipes cleaned, there's Marianne's place down the street. In my house, though, you're a good boy or you're out on your ass, you got that?"

"Yes, ma'am," I said, smartly.

"Don't get me wrong. I'm no prude. No prude could live in this place five minutes. But we all do what we believe in . . . And I've got this notion that we're going to be a town someday, a real town . . . What you see out there today isn't real. This is just a phase, a stage. It's a kid's dream where naughty boys can come and play their games. But it won't last. It can't. Or that's how I'm betting. And if I'm right, I'm going to be one of the richest women in New Mexico . . . "

"And if you're wrong?" I asked.

She shrugged. "We don't get to choose, do we? It's a matter not so much of conviction as taste. Inclination. Your life is what you do with it, what you make of it, which is the only way you ever find out who you are."

"That certainly is true," I agreed. "How much is the room?"

She explained that she had two different prices, one for tourists and trouble-makers, another for residents. Residents, it turned out, were those who had jobs in Hotdog. Did I have a job? Or, more to the point, did I want one? Doing chores, cutting firewood, sweeping up, helping with the laundry when the Indian woman didn't show up?

"Sure, why not?" I said. It was the kind of welcome a man isn't likely to get very often, and I was grateful for it. "I've got nothing else in particular in my appointment book."

"It'll fill up, I have no doubt," she promised.

I took the room as a resident, and on a week-to-week deal. She nodded gravely, then said, "Welcome to Hotdog" and pumped my hand a couple of times, making it official.

It's more than I'd had in a lot of places, more than a man is likely to get, I'll tell you, in a lot of towns that think of themselves as civilized.

II

THERE'S NO SUCH THING AS REALITY. What you think of as real, what you take as the benchmark, is what you're used to. Which is a sloppy way of saying the obvious truth that reality is just a fancy label for the habitual and the familiar. And we are creatures of habit, each and every one of us, even in a place like Hotdog. Even Sodom and Gomorra must have had their routines, their daily rounds of sin and orgy, of sodomy and . . . whatever it was they were up to in Gomorra.

In Hotdog, too, there were routines, ways of getting through the day, some more entertaining or relaxing, and others more strenuous or disagreeable. Post-hole digging, for example, was a sweaty way to make a dollar. Prospecting for turquoise was a kind of gamble, but if the weather was nice, what you got was a pleasant ride out into the hills. You might come back with some stones, or maybe a jack-rabbit for the stew pot. Or even a deer. Or you could have nothing to show for your troubles but a saddle-sore rump. Still, it was something to do, and it allowed you to kid yourself into thinking you deserved an evening in the Black Garter or a half hour with one of the girls down the street at Marianne's place.

My point isn't to justify or defend the way we were living, but only to assert that that's how it was, and that it seemed, after a while, perfectly normal, natural, and predictable. It was what we took for granted, what we assumed, what we thought of as real. It doesn't take any genius to figure this out — but only an intellectual would wonder about it, would speculate as to whether these assumptions about daily life weren't absolutely arbitrary. Was it necessary to live as we did? Was it a stage or a phase, as Julie thought, or only a lack of alternatives?

Or, putting it another way, did our lack of alternatives come from anything but our own poverty of imagination? There we were, unhemmed, unbounded, the freest men and women in the world, with those grand and empty expanses rolling away to make you gasp with their spaciousness, the desert on one side and the hills on the other, and we were as confined in our notions of how to live as chickens in a coop. All of us, that is, except the Duke — who was thinking, as Claude had warned me that first day I'd come into town.

All we knew was that one day Marianne and her girls were gone. The place was still there, an empty building for us to stare at as if to reassure ourselves that we hadn't been the victims of mass hysteria, sharing some collective wet-dream. All that giggling nookie had packed up and skedaddled, back down to Santa Fe. There were all kinds of guesses about what had happened, the most optimistic view being that Marianne had just gone down to trade in the old whores for a new crew. But why wouldn't she have announced this? Why wouldn't she have proclaimed it, if only for the sake of business? In that odd outpost of humanity, there were relationships for which it is difficult to find easy descriptions or models in literature, connections that some of us felt to some of the girls — nothing like love, I admit, but a partiality, or even, say, a fondness. Who wouldn't have dropped in for a good-bye screw? Marianne could have had herself a fine old house party. At the very least, knowing that we'd be left without female companionship for a week or so, there'd have been a number of us who would have come by for hygienic reasons, to try to prevent excessive goatiness.

But just gone? Snuck off in the middle of the night? We required some explanation, some reassurance that cause-and-effect was still an operating principle, even out here on the banks of the turgid Gila River. And we found our answer at the Black Garter, where Angel allowed as how there had been a ruckus down at Marianne's the night before, that some lonely cowboy in with one of the girls had refused to admit that he just couldn't get it up for the third time. Meanwhile, some even lonelier cowboy out in the hall got tired of the conversation he couldn't help hearing through the transom, decided that it was tasteless, boring, an abuse of the girl's hospitality, and, more to the point, a dog-in-the-manger waste of the girl's time, for which he had, himself, better ideas. He voiced these thoughts, but the guy in the bed took umbrage. He also took his revolver out of the holster he had slung over the back of a chair, and came out to answer what he had taken to be an impertinence.

If the fellow in the hallway hadn't laughed at him and suggested that there probably weren't any bullets in the gun either, the first lonely cowboy might have been content to brandish his weapon and bluster a bit. But he had been called on his manliness — twice in as many minutes — and he shot the other lonely cowboy right between the eyes.

"Bad for business," Angel said. "Bad for the town. Bad for the territory. The Duke was real mad."

And where was the Duke? For the first time, we realized that he too was nowhere to be seen.

"Yeah, he's gone," Angel said, "but just for a while. A couple of weeks, maybe. He's taken the girls to Santa Fe."

"Helping Marianne pick the next bunch?" somebody asked.

"Trying them out," somebody else suggested. "Auditioning them, as it were."

Angel didn't answer. He just stood there, drying an already bone-dry shot glass with his none too clean dish towel.

"What is it you're not telling us?" Claude asked him.

"The Duke has decided to clean up the town. We're going legit."

"What? What are you talking about?"

"No more whores," Angel said.

"What the fuck!" Claude said, and then, "I think I need a drink." And he wasn't the only one.

*　*　*

Was Angel serious? Was he just jerking us around, or was the Duke? Or was this an authentic if nutty vision, a grand scheme worthy of comparison with those of the greatest thinkers, Plato, say, or Thomas More? I mean, look at it from the common-sense angle and you see that there was no profit in it for the Duke if he cleaned up Hotdog. He ran the saloon and made money from the drinking and the gambling. He either owned the whore house that Marianne ran, or else he got some kind of rake-off from her, protection money at least. Or could have, if he'd wanted to. But he'd decided, like that, out of the blue sky — of which we have plenty out here, a limitless vertiginous expanse of it — that Hotdog should be turned into a suburb of the City of God. Some crude cowpoke gets himself shot for being a damnfool and impatient, and the Duke was going to take this as a sign from on high that we should all pull up our socks, or at least button our pants?

The Good Book tells us how to live, Angel reminded us, and now it would no longer be an empty statement of the ideal, but a simple declaration of the law. Which the Duke had promulgated, and which, in the Duke's absence, he, Angel, would enforce.

Guffaws, of course, even a few derisive hoots of laughter, but not a rise out of Angel, no sudden rictus to let us know that, of course, it was a joke, however bizarre and tasteless.

The trouble with Angel's explanation was, first of all, that it was nuts. This had hardly been the first awkward moment down at Marianne's leaping academy, or even the first contretemps to have resulted in bloodshed. The problem wasn't at Marianne's place but in the Duke's head. This shooting hadn't been the cause of his decision — not even the final straw — but only the cue, the signal for which he had been waiting. The way we were living was wrong, and an abomination . . .

"A what?" Claude asked. "You've got to be fucking kidding."

"A-bom-in-a-tion!" Angel repeated, one syllable at a time. It wasn't a word in his usual range, but that was disturbing because what it meant was that somebody had taught it to him. Somebody he either feared enough or respected enough so that he'd bothered to learn it.

"A-bom-in-a-tion!" Claude repeated. "Unto the Lord?"

"That's right," Angel said, brightening. "That's just what he said."

I suppose that if I'd been smarter, I might have guessed my first day here that this could happen. The hints had been there, or call them signs and portents if you want to. Claude's information that the Duke was an intellectual, and the discussion at dinner about Grace, horses, heaven, and all that foolishness was as good as a pillar of cloud in the desert, or even a pillar of fire. But who can draw a conclusion from such evidence and then, with assurance, act on it? It was only in retrospect that these things emerged in rubric, clarifying their significance and mocking us for our obtuseness.

What we thought at the time was that, sure, for a while the Duke would have his little game. We'd have a town without any whores, and business would fall off. The town would die, maybe. Or the Duke would get bored and relent. Or move on and leave us to our own devices. Or perhaps we would move on and leave him and Angel to rot in their bizarre utopia out in the wilderness. But who could take such far-fetched ideas seriously? It had to be a joke, some elaborate prank that would demonstrate the Duke's power yet still end up with a wagonload of new ladies from Santa Fe, every bit as juicy, giggly, sultry, brassy, and extravagant as the last batch. And the abstinence of a week or two would turn out to have whetted our appetites so that we would be all the more enthusiastic in our welcomes to our new hostesses at Marianne's.

In that case, all the nonsense Angel was spouting was just part of the game. The stuff about lechery and the vileness of fornication. "As it is written, 'If a man is found lying with the wife of another man, both of them shall die, the man who lay with the woman, and the woman; so you shall purge the evil from Israel.' Deuteronomy, twenty-two: twenty-two."

"You have got to be out of your pussy-loving mind," Claude remarked, quietly but firmly.

Angel didn't seem to take it as an insult. He went on

citing scripture: "'Do not defile yourselves by any of these
things, for by all these the nations I am casting out before you
defiled themselves; and the land became defiled, so that I
punished its iniquity, and the land vomited out its inhabit-
ants. But you shall keep my statutes and my ordinances and
do none of these abominations, either the native or the
stranger who sojourns among you.' Leviticus, eighteen:
twenty-four!"

"What's that?" Gaspard wanted to know.

"It's a book of the Bible," Claude informed him. "But it
sure is odd for this ignorant son-of-a-bitch to be spouting the
Bible at us like that. Angel, how did you do that?" he asked.

"I got it written down here on these little cards the Duke
left for me," Angel admitted readily enough.

And by Christ he did!

*   *   *

We were outraged. What the hell was this? The whole idea
of the West, for God's sake, is to be free to do what you want,
to know that nobody's going to be sticking his nose into your
business, to take advantage of all that space and discover not
just another hillside or arroyo but the truth of the human
terrain, the possibilities that are hard to find in cities except
in back alleys where the smell of corruption taints everything
with itself. Here, in the fresh air, under the open skies, we
could invent ourselves afresh, figuring out as we went along
what worked and what didn't.

And suddenly, in defiance of nature — one might even
say, of nature's laws — the Duke had decreed that the whore
house should cease to operate. He wanted us to remake
ourselves not even in his image, but rather according to his

cerebrated and calculated scheme of how things ought to be. Wurst would be best, and the devil take the hintermost. Hotdog! But no more buns.

Such were the remarks that were more or less predictable. To which, I confess, I added my own two cents' worth. "A bad idea," I said, "for perfectly obvious physiological reasons. The cowboy who spends all that time in the saddle experiences a testicular stimulation from the very business of riding. His seminal vesicles are effervescent with the relentless stimulation, and he is therefore hornier than the ordinary laborer. His needs for sexual release are, as it were, more pressing."

Claude laughed, and Gaspard, and some of the others. But Angel had his instructions, and he was so full of himself and his new authority that he wasn't going to risk so much as a small conspiratorial smile. We could blather on as much as we liked, but it would do us no goddamn good.

Well, we grumbled, of course, and we were well and truly pissed off . . . But when it comes to the great subjects — like Good, Evil, the Meaning of Life, and Nookie — everyone's sort of ambivalent. I mean, the Duke's peremptoriness was annoying, but there was something to be said for having a town that wasn't just a glory hole in the desert.

We may be creatures of the flesh, but we are not solely that. We have our grand and lofty notions, even if these can be as embarrassing to us as a sudden hard-on at a high-school dance. We had none of us been born and bred in this peculiar place, but each had come to it fleeing something or craving something . . . Or, putting it more bluntly, we had our wounds and troubles, and everyone knew this — which made it less likely that we'd be willing to confess about what hurt. Far better to play the part of the tough hombre who cares for nothing and no one, who may want to get his rocks off from time to time, but is not likely to admit a need for understanding, sympathy, affection, companionship, or anything like it.

The ordinary courtesies by which a man will open a door for a woman, or stand up if she should rise from her chair — these had been observed only in the breach, defied, one might say, as sissy-boy stuff and nonsense in which we no longer believed. In a town whose livelihood depended in such large measure on whores and whoring, it was awkward for anyone to admit to these almost unmanly feelings. But is it ever unmanly to draw a chair from the table and hold it so that a lady may sit down? Is it unmanly to hear a woman's weeping in the small hours of the night and feel prompted to come to her aid, to protect her, to save her from a savagery and beastliness all too easy for one to imagine because one has seen it often enough with one's own eyes? At the very least, what manner of man can avoid at such times a pang of guilt at his own helplessness and cowardice?

I am extrapolating from my own thoughts to those of the other men in town, but not too fancifully or too far, I think. We grumbled, then, at the new dispensation, protested loudly that this sudden clean-up of Hotdog was a zany idea that couldn't possibly last, but at least in some of our minds there were some doubts, perhaps even some hopes.

We managed to stagger through those first few delicate days, and I found myself thinking that this was the interesting thing about being human — that we could adapt, that we could reorient ourselves to a changed environment. Break old habits, and after a while new ones will come to replace them, as arbitrary perhaps as the previous set, but functional. It is not too extravagant to claim that the Duke's decree had changed the entire environment, and that these changes manifested themselves in surprising ways. We still played poker at the Black Garter, but suddenly the stakes were much smaller. Who knows why? Maybe we weren't showing off to each other anymore, as if being tough and macho at the table were the equivalent of a similar run of luck later on in one of Marianne's bedrooms, as if one was either a token or else a substitute for the other. Or maybe the guys were just saving their money for a trip into Santa Fe, which there was now more reason to undertake.

What am I trying to say here? Or afraid of saying? I'll come right out and level with you. The point is that sometimes I wonder whether it might not have worked. If things had gone just a little bit differently, it could have been a great thing, nothing less than a social revolution, however small in scale. And as I tell the rest of this sorry story, you have to keep that in mind: that it wasn't necessarily the theory that was wrong, and that, with a little more finesse, a little more tact and shrewdness in execution, it could have goddamn worked! Which is the tricky thing always about history, as you're reading it or writing it. This happened and then this happened. . . But did the second thing follow necessarily from the first? Couldn't there have been other outcomes, either better or worse, or absolutely different? Does the fact that this is how the hand played out mean that it's likely to happen again?

It beats the hell out of me. But I'd be dishonest if I didn't at least admit to moments of gratitude and assent. Skeptical? Of course I was. We all were. And annoyed at the inconvenience and at the implied criticism that, until the Duke's sudden moment of illumination, we'd all been living like a bunch of pigs and low-lifes. Well, nobody likes to be told a thing like that, and never so peremptorily. But there was a

compliment, too, in his decree: that we were capable of something more and better. What he was implying was that we,
the citizens of Hotdog, and indeed all mankind, were capable
of improvement, if not perfection.

There was surely room for improvement. As Angel
demonstrated only a couple of nights later.

There were ringing bells, gunshots . . . It was a hell of a
racket, just like in the bad old days, but with at least one
significant difference. The Duke's goons, who were supposed
to keep order or at least keep disorder from getting altogether
out of hand, had continued to prowl the streets at night. The
difference is that in the absence of any interesting mischief
they could legitimately occupy themselves restraining, they
were turning their scrutiny upon the pursuits and diversions
of those who, in Hotdog anyway, were the good guys, the
decent, respectable, law-abiding folks.

To get down to it, these vigilantes had discovered Claude
climbing down the trellis outside Julie's bedroom.

Funny, right? Embarrassing, even. An awkward and
comical piece of business, but of no real consequence. One
wouldn't have thought so, except that you can never tell what
will happen when you take an underling and give him a little
authority, a little power. It's a heady drug that affects some
people in very strange ways. Angel, whom the Duke had left
in charge of things, took it as an affront to his dignity and
office that fornication was going on, in his town on his watch.
And in defiance of the Duke's orders.

Which was total horse-shit! The Duke, as we argued, all
of us that night who were lodgers in Julie's house, and everyone in town the next day, hadn't been trying to prohibit
fornication, which was a bizarre thought. He'd just wanted
to stop the whoring, which is sex for money. No money had

changed hands. This was sport-fucking, a friendly tussle of mutually consenting adults . . .

It is tedious to recite the arguments when they're so obvious. But we went through the whole boring exercise, many times in fact, and got absolutely nowhere.

"Fornication," Angel pronounced, and the penalty was . . . He flipped pages in his Bible, read a chapter here and a verse there, running along the words with his fingertip the way people do who aren't really comfortable with reading, and came up at last with "Death."

"For both of them?" Gaspard asked.

"Nah! Just Claude," Angel said. And then to Claude he said, "Sorry, old buddy, but . . . we're going to have to hang you."

"Have to?" Claude asked, not particularly excited. He couldn't believe what was happening, what he was hearing.

"As an example to the others," Angel said, shaking his head. And you'd have thought from the way Claude nodded his head that he was satisfied with the reasonableness of this explanation.

He was still nodding, I swear, as the goons hustled him down the street toward the jailhouse.

III

HORSE PLAY, OF COURSE — or so Claude supposed. But they really did lock him up, and then, from his cell window, he could see that they really were setting up the gallows out there in the street. It began to sink in that, even if this had started as a piece of buffoonery, somebody ought to stop it before sheer momentum carried it all just a little too far.

People have died for the stupidest reasons. In the French Revolution, for instance, Lavoisier got beheaded for having invented the whoopee cushion (a legitimate by-product of his researches into separation of gasses — a visitor to his lab sat on one of his gas-bags and made that sublimely vulgar noise) and for having scattered them around in the assembly chamber, not neglecting to provide one for Robespierre's very own seat.

Off with his head, they said, and whether it started out as a bon mot, it ended up on the guillotine, with the great chemist's actual head getting lopped off and falling into the basket, as the crowd, ever discriminating, always fair and proper and just, cheered their lungs out.

People talked to Angel — Julie, of course, and Gaspard, and some of the others. I tried talking to him myself, but he had his instructions, he said, and that was the end of it. In which case, the only thing was for someone to go off to Santa Fe and try to find A) the Duke, B) the Federal Marshal, C) the U. S. Cavalry, or D) any gunfighter willing to come back and put Angel in his place, intimidating him if that was possible, or killing him if it came to that. As Julie's not-quite-hired hand, I was the likely candidate.

Off to Santa Fe? Two days' ride? That's four days, really, but a man could do it in a day and a night down, and then get back in another day and a night of exhausting, bone-jarring effort.

"Please," Julie said. "You've got to."

I couldn't think of any other prospect. And it wasn't the kind of thing a woman was going to do by herself.

"Sure," I agreed, producing a kind of smile at the ridiculousness of my luck — Claude, who had got himself laid, would get to lounge around in a comfortable cell, while I, who had nothing to do with any of this and wasn't even *from* here, would have to drag ass down to the capital of the territory, hoping to find help. Sanity. Relief.

"Oh yes, and while you're there. . . " Julie said.

What else, I wondered. Pick up some hair curlers? Baking powder? Cold cream? But it wasn't anything like that.

"Claude's got a sister in Santa Fe. Isabel. You might try to find her. She could help, maybe. She'd be at the mission."

"Okay," I said, a little ashamed of myself.

Of course, what I should have been doing instead of acting dumb was pay attention, for instance to that remark about how I'd be likely to find her at the mission.

It didn't register until hours later, when I was out there on the trail. But even then, I supposed she would be a teacher or maybe a cleaning woman. It never crossed my mind that Claude's sister would turn out to be a fucking nun.

*   *   *

Do nuns give you the willies? Do you suppose that you must be some special kind of monster to be uneasy about them, to imagine them, despite all your resolutions to cut it out for Christ's sake, in all kinds of sordid sexual excess? Well, you're not alone. Look at Diderot, or indeed at that whole sub-genre of ecclesiastical pornography. You're not crazy, not even original. It is a common, ordinary and, if you'll excuse me for saying so, perfectly reasonable fantasy to entertain, because the main thing about being a nun is that they don't get laid. They have abjured sex. And why on earth would they have chosen sex to abjure if they didn't understand its importance, if they weren't possessed by lusts stronger than those of most women. If they are "offering it up" as a sacrifice to God's glory, or for the benefit of the souls in purgatory, or on whatever other bizarre theological or eschatological pretext, you can reasonably infer that this is the most important thing they can imagine. And so they do imagine it, you bet your ass (or theirs!). They go around in a semi-rapture, like those Chinese sybarites with the ben-wah balls stuck up their twats, so that every step they take is masturbatory. Look at the face of St. Theresa, as Bernini has carved it, and try to explain it as anything other than a sexual sizzle.

They love it! The authentic ones do. There are some, I guess, who are there because their families stuck them away, ugly and unmarriageable, or too poor for dowries, or disobedient, or crazy, or in some other way inconvenient. But the ones with what they call an authentic vocation are there because they are hot, because they love fucking so much that it scares them, and in terror or self-loathing or despair they have fled to these nunneries, which are God's whore houses. There they can do penance, get up in the middle of the night to pray, kneel on the hard floor, prostrate themselves before the altar, mortify the flesh, and seek salvation . . .

So, no, you're not crazy having thought such things. If anything, you're short of the mark, because the nuns are the ones who see sex everywhere, who see the world as if it were full of stiff pizzles quivering in excitement and aimed right at them. Your only error is to have pushed away such thoughts, dismissing them as grotesque and perverse when you don't know the first thing about perversion. But still that's what we do, blame ourselves. Or what I did, at any rate, when I got to Santa Fe. And that was a big mistake.

Looking up Isabel was not the main reason for my trip, of course, but it was something to do after I had searched for the Duke without any success. No word of him, nothing! And Santa Fe back then was a really small town, not the kind of place where a guy like the Duke wouldn't have been noticed. If he'd been there, somebody would have seen him — the bartenders, or the marshal, or the people at the livery stable.

I tried the whore houses too, figuring that this bizarre business back in Hotdog might have some connection with his visit to Santa Fe, but nobody had seen him or heard from him or expected him to show up. Very mysterious, I thought.

I considered for maybe twenty seconds going to the marshal's office. But not yet. How did I know what the relation was between the marshal and the Duke. The first thing to do was talk to Isabel, who'd been here a while and might have some idea whom to trust. And I could find her easily enough.

She was up at the mission, at the convent to be precise, and was at the point of joining the order — a novice or a postulant or whatever you call them before they make their vows. Only a couple of days later and she wouldn't have been able to leave, not even to try to save her brother's life.

She was wearing the costume, the habit I guess you'd call it, with the wimple and all. But under all that cloth, I could see that she was a good-looking woman, which oughtn't to have been so surprising. Maybe her view of the world wasn't so skewed then, and maybe men had been coming on to her all the time . . . In which case, what she was running away from could either have been all those men, or it could as easily have been her own delight in their attention, which was even tougher to live with. But the habit framed her looks, played you a game of peek-a-boo, so that you looked very carefully at a tiny visible wisp of *chatain* hair that was more striking in its effect than if she'd been bare headed. I caught myself wondering about what the rest of her hair looked like . . .

And I thought that hookers, if they were smart, would dress themselves like nuns.

And I realized that, of course, some of them, being smart, do.

But her mildly hostile greeting was enough to get my mind back to business. "What urgent matter?" she asked. "Who are you?" These were clearly perfunctory and dismissive questions she hoped I would have no satisfactory answers for, in which case she could then retreat to the inner chambers of the convent.

"Your brother is in jail," I told her. "And there's a good chance that he might actually be hanged. You've got to come back with me to Hotdog to try to help him."

"I can't imagine what I could do."

"Okay," I said. "In that case, I've delivered the message. I'll tell him what you said."

"You're . . . you're serious? In jail? Hanged?"

I nodded and then explained, as well as I could, what had happened.

She agreed to come with me. Not that she was sure there was anything she could do. Nor was I, for that matter. But to tell the truth, I had failed to find the Duke, and I was glad to have her along with me to show that I'd tried, that I'd made it to Santa Fe. It was better to come back with her than with nobody.

As we had plenty of time to talk on the way back, I began to wonder whether she mightn't be worse than useless, whether she wouldn't even turn out to be an advocate against her brother's cause. "It's odd," she said, "my having to speak up for Claude this way . . . "

"Why's that?" I asked her.

"If it weren't my brother, I'd be in favor of what they're trying to do. These towns have to be cleaned up. It's a good idea, a good impulse. They're doing what's right."

She went on at some length about how morality was exactly what this territory needed. And she even agreed that the best way to get the attention of the people was to come down hard on a few exemplary malefactors, like her brother for instance.

"You want to pull the handle on him?" I asked her. "You want to spring the trap yourself? You talk to Angel that way and that's just about what you'll be doing."

There was a long silence. I mean some ten or fifteen minutes. What had I done? Or was this some kind of strategy she was working out, a way of getting to Angel, of seeming to agree with him and the Duke, so that her plea for mercy might carry more weight?

The thing about the West is that it isn't subtle. There

are these long vistas, and you can tell pretty much where you are. Mountains. Deserts. Prairies. Think about it. They're all huge, enormous, and they come on to you as if you were an uncooperative mule and God was trying to get your attention by hitting you between the eyes with a two-by-four. Subtlety and nuance are for back East.

"I'm sure there must be a way of straightening it out," she said, as if we hadn't been quiet all that time, or maybe it's that nuns have a different sense of time from the rest of us. "If Claude and the woman were to marry, that would be acceptable to all parties, I should think."

This was not such an arcane idea that Julie and Claude hadn't already thought of it. And that Angel hadn't already rejected it. But I didn't say anything. Maybe with her nun's suit on and those wisps of hair coming out of the headgear, the Duke's stern lieutenant might soften a little. Or the impressiveness of her starchy piety might do the trick, getting him at least to hesitate, postponing the execution until the Duke returned to town.

But it wasn't a bet I would have wanted to stake my life on.

What's hard to reckon, when you're dealing with people who are all crazy as bedbugs — which is most of us, most of the time — is what's going to sound persuasive to them.

"You're new in Hotdog, aren't you?" she asked.

I told her I was. She'd lived there, after all, until just a few months before. And of course she had hated it because it was just a bar and a whore house pretending to be a town. She'd come with her brother. Their parents had died a couple of years before and he'd wanted to go west and try to strike it rich. She had tried to discourage him and failed, and her choice, she realized, had been between letting him go off alone — to hell and damnation, of course — and going along with him, to continue as well as they could together and act as if they were still a family.

It's a long way, though, from discovering that Hotdog wasn't where she wanted to live to deciding to lock herself away in a nunnery, but the right moment never presented itself in which I could ask about this with any grace. I just figured that craziness manifests itself in a wild variety of ways, and there was also the possibility — remote but, still, a possibility — that she'd had some kind of sudden vocation, or whatever it is they call it. The call, I guess. Maybe it was a kind of spiritual agoraphobia, all of the West's open space turning into an intimidation, or a burden, or even an accusation.

We rode until dusk, made camp, were up before dawn, and then rode all the next day, getting to Hotdog late in the afternoon. Mostly she was silent, and I let her alone, hoping that she might put the time to good use, thinking, or scheming, or maybe just psyching herself up. There is a respect that even a wise-ass like me feels for someone else's troubles.

We came over the last rise, and looked down into the valley at the puny line of buildings. It struck me at that moment that what I ought to have done back in Santa Fe was ask her if she had any money. With a couple of hundred bucks, she could have hired herself a set of thugs to come riding into town and spring old Claude . . . But that's not the kind of thing one suggests to a nun, for God's sake.

But with the Duke out of town, she might very well have been able to bring it off!

* * *

I had done what I'd promised. If I hadn't been able to find the Duke, I had brought Isabel back to Hotdog. It wasn't any of my business now what happened. I was just there, one of the crowd you might say, and if I had friendly feelings toward old Claude and didn't want to see him strung up for such a damn-fool reason as fornication, there was also a part of me that was eager to see confirmed in so dramatic a way my worst suspicions about . . . The world? Mankind? The human condition? Whatever. It wasn't *Schadenfreude*, that nasty satisfaction you take in a friend's misfortunes, but the confirmation of a more general sense of the woefulness of things. It's as if Angel weren't just some crazy scarfaced bartender but an actual messenger of the Lord, or perhaps of the Devil, come to deliver his annunciation: "Fear not, it isn't you. You're not depressed or nuts in any way. This is real, and the gloom you feel is correct and appropriate."

I don't know a name for the assurance one takes from such a happening. But in this approximate and inefficient way, I have tried to suggest how and why a part of me was looking forward, philosophically, metaphysically, to seeing Claude hanged — as were the others in town.

I took Isabel back to Julie's place. I was looking forward to a hot bath to ease my saddle-sore ass and then a nice long snooze, and I was surprised when Isabel asked me to take her down to the Black Garter.

"What for?" I should have asked. "It's just down the street. You can see it from here. You don't need me. I can't be of any more help to you. If anything, my coming along will only make it harder for you, because if you can get Angel even to begin thinking about changing his mind, which I doubt, my presence — or anybody's for that matter — is only going to make it harder for him to back down."

That's what I should have said. I thought it, could see it just as if it were written out for me to recite. But what the hell, there she was, this nun, or less-than-nun, asking me to walk a hundred yards down the street so she wouldn't have to walk into the bar all by herself. Not such a big thing, right?

I'd just ridden for four days to bring her back to Hotdog, a grand or stupid gesture, and I wasn't prepared to forgo all the credit, even in my own mind. And that was exactly what would have happened if I'd told her to haul her ass down to the Black Garter and not gone along with her myself.

"Surely," is what I heard coming out of my own mouth, as if I'd been taken over by some supernatural spirit the way the Indians say can happen to anyone at almost any time. And then, because I'd already lost the prospect of that immediate bath and nap, and I figured I could reschedule my rewards and make it a drink, a bath, and a nap, I even added, "Be glad to."

We left Julie to see to the horses and went on down to see what Isabel could do to get Angel to lighten up on Claude. She didn't even stop to wash up or anything, which only made it more dramatic.

You don't often see in a bar in a western town a nun with a wimple walking in through the double doors, trailing white linen as if it were a cloud of glory. And the sweat and the dirt from the trail only highlit the urgency of her appearance there. The way she came bursting in, she had his attention right away, believe me. For a moment, I even allowed myself a flicker of hope that she might persuade him . . . at least to wait a while. And he did something I'd never seen him do before, which was to invite her back into the "office."

A grand word for it, but then Hotdog was full of grand words. If architecture is expensive, grandiloquence is fairly

cheap. What Angel meant in this instance was the little alcove
in the store room where the Duke had a desk at which he
could do the accounts, write out orders for supplies, make up
pay packets, and perform the other clerical business that was
involved in running the Black Garter. There was a desk, a
chair, and another chair, in which Isabel sat.

Or maybe she stood, walking back and forth.

How the hell do I know? I mean, this part of it I have
to put together from what he told me, what she told me, what
I know about each of them, and what happened later. And
it's hard to imagine. Hell, it must have been hard to imagine
for them, too, even as they were going through it. She was
there to plead for Claude's life, although she agreed with the
basic nutty idea that fornication had to be stopped, that
Hotdog had to be cleaned up, and even that a hanging or two
was an efficient way to get this difficult job done quickly and,
for the rest of the town, painlessly. A sacrificial lamb, or goat,
or whatever barnyard beast Claude was going to be, wasn't
such a bad thing if the cause was good enough.

As, for Christ's sweet sake, she thought it was!

This must have taken poor Angel by some surprise. It
wasn't a quarter from which he'd have expected anyone to
attack. And those wisps of hair could have got to him. This
is altogether irrational and doesn't allow for any kind of
explanation, but my guess is that he was smitten instantly,
utterly taken with her. A sweaty nun is not an image you see
often on calendars and in girlie magazines, but then maybe
you just aren't looking in the right places. There are all kinds
of refined tastes, aren't there?

I mean, let's face it. That riff a while back about nuns
wasn't altogether a joke. I mean, seriously, what man hasn't
supposed himself to be . . . beastly, a depraved and foul crea-

ture eager to soil the very thing he adores, to force the woman he loves to submit to the passions of which he is, himself, deeply ashamed. The idea of the purity and loftiness of woman is very likely a projection that draws its energy from this self-hatred and disgust. But there it is, the worship of the pure and chaste woman . . . for whom a unicorn would die (and deserves to, actually, with that great phallic protuberance coming out of his forehead). Think of the story about Beauty and the Beast, which celebrates the self-loathing all men feel and most men have, at one time or another, dredged up from their psychic depths to confront. So to get a nun to submit to you, to get her to rip off her wimple and the rest of her elaborate habit, to get her to play out your dirtiest and most extravagant fantasies is to get an acceptance of your passions you couldn't begin to imagine on your own. And she can forgive you for fucking her, even as it is happening. If she can forgive you, maybe you can begin to forgive yourself; if she can share your guilt, then perhaps it won't be so heavy a burden.

But you get the idea. The point is that, somehow or other, in that little cubby hole in the store room while they were discussing their complicated series of inextricable problems, it became clear to both of them what the deal was. If she wanted Angel not to hang Claude for fornication, not to make him pay for sex with death, then, in this grotesque arbitrage, she would have to redeem the death with the only other coin of this rarefied realm, which is to say, sex. Tit for tat and measure for measure. Angel would spare her brother if Isabel would lie down and let Angel do the old rumpy-pumpy with her.

It'd make a hell of an opera, wouldn't it? But all that means is that there was an extravagance, even a kind of daring, in the vision of that equation. It wasn't what you see every day of the week, especially in a shit-hole like Hotdog. And the wild thing was that it suited Isabel exactly.

She who had been driven to that goddamned nunnery by the idea of all those penises pointing at her comes back out for one last good deed, and what does she get but a crude and distasteful proposition from a beaner bartender with a scar on his cheek and delusions of grandeur, which are always more dangerous than a mid-day desert sun?

She was . . . not surprised. After all that thinking on the road, this was pretty much what she'd expected, and perhaps even what she'd wanted, and she knew how to react, which was cautiously. She didn't want to look too eager. She wanted to make him think it was a very big deal, because that was the whole point of it. She had to at least play hard to get, right?

"I'll consider it," she said.

Cloistered nun, back-alley whore, or Mistress In-Between, isn't that what they all say?

*   *   *

A done deal, then, right? She wants it, and he wants it, and down the street in the pokey Claude is, if you'll pardon the expression, hanging on their every word, gesture, sigh, and look. The rest of us in Hotdog are reassured to see that what we recognize as the human condition looks to be on its way back It isn't necessarily admirable, but it's familiar, normal, and known. Pretensions at extraordinary virtue are like soap bubbles floating in the air, shiny as jewels, but it's just a matter of seconds before they pop and set you down once again in the sin and corruption that was there all along.

All we had to do was wait for them to work it out, how and where and when and in what positions, and then Claude and all the rest of us could breathe easier and get on with our lives. Not that Isabel had actually indicated that she'd do the dirty with the bartender, but what kind of question could there be? Particularly if she called herself a Christian, right? You save the poor innocent. You are your brother's keeper. You get to make jig-a-jig and you don't even have to assume the guilt of it, because you're doing it for an unimpeachably humanitarian reason.

Right? Well of course! And Isabel's hesitation was just for show, so that we'd appreciate her fucking sacrifice! She was thinking — or said she was, at any rate — that dishonor was worse than death. That her brother ought to be willing to die to save her chastity. And if he wasn't willing and even eager to do this little thing for her, to undergo a few minutes of discomfort before meeting his maker, then he was no kind of a brother, and not worth bothering with and . . . let him go hang, as the expression so aptly goes. In a weird way, the more worthless the brother was, the more generous and worthy the sister's sacrifice for him became.

What she wanted was permission and, even more than that, urging and, on top of that, admiration. From the world and heaven, too. She wanted to do exactly what she'd dreamed of, but to have us all understand that it was only reluctantly and to save her worthless sibling. And we'd have been able to play this out convincingly enough, if Brother Luis hadn't shown up.

Brother Luis? Well, maybe if you were blind, and deaf, and retarded too, you might have been fooled for a while. But anyone else could see that the elaborate monk's habit with the huge hood that covered most of his face was out of a costume shop. Or no, not even that persuasive; it looked to be home-made. The rope ceinture and the too new sandals were odd looking, but the huge hood was the give-away. And the voice, of course. It was clear to the least observant man or woman in the entire New Mexico Territory that, for whatever bizarre reasons, the Duke was back, having disguised himself as a monk. He was having himself a good time.

Which meant, obviously, that Claude was no longer in any real danger. We were having a kind of charade here, a parlor game into which the whole town had been recruited.

Which was, after all, a brilliant idea!

The point had been to clean up Hotdog. Get the whores out of town, establish a Chamber of Commerce, a Better Business Bureau, a Town Watch, and all that machinery of bourgeois respectability, because that was the key to the golden door to a prosperous future . . . Opportunity and responsibility! Progress through co-operation and respect. Equal justice under law. All those grand phrases.

How to improve Hotdog? Well, I guess the Duke could have actually done what we thought he had done: get out of town and leave Angel and the goons to hang a couple of malefactors chosen more or less at random. Or, in a more humane way, he could just pretend to be doing that, making the same point dramatically but bloodlessly. The shadow can work as well as the real thing, sometimes.

There was also an element of intellectual play in it, a philosophical kind of fun and games, which made the charade not only more gentle but more . . . interesting. And why not? The thing about running a town that way, about having power, is that it gets to be interesting. If you are one of those intellectuals, you start wondering what the limits are of your powers, or of any human powers. What is the human condition, and what can you do to change it?

A whole lot of fairly abstruse questions were whirling around in the dry desert air, I'd be willing to bet, and as had happened so often with real dukes, our Duke's aptitudes weren't quite adequate to these lofty exercises in philosophical inquiry.

But there he was . . . Or, abruptly, and from out of nowhere, there was this improbable figure of Brother Luis, a monk who kept his face covered, who seemed unwilling to show himself much around town, and who looked and sounded a whole lot like the Duke we all knew and feared. Which is why nobody said, "Hey, cut the crap, Brother, we know who you are, you ridiculous son-of-a bitch . . . " If he wasn't the Duke, then that would have been rude and irreverent, and if he was, then it would have been dangerous. If he wanted to be Brother Luis, or Napoleon Bonaparte, or Humpty-Dumpty, then that was fine with the rest of us.

This didn't mean, however, that one couldn't kid him a little.

We told him what was going on . . . it was, as you'd expect, the only topic of conversation in town. And he wanted to know what kind of man the Duke was who could have put such a peculiar plan into effect.

I took it to be an opportunity. He was playing his game, and it seemed only right that some of us should get to make side bets. "What would you expect of a guy who owns the only saloon in town?" I asked the good friar.

"What do you mean?"

"He waters his drinks," I said. "He's a thief."

Silence, but a satisfactory glare.

"He's also a hypocrite," I suggested, as if I'd just now figured this out.

The friar looked furious, but couldn't say anything. He did manage to ask, "Oh! Why?"

"Well, he's a whoremaster, and a great fucker-around," I said. "Or he used to be. A cocksman of the first water. But then he had a change of heart, or more likely some other, smaller part of him. And if he couldn't have any, then he wasn't going to stand around while his neighbors were getting it. So he decided to clean up the town. A devout hypocrite and an utter villain, and. . ."

The monk put up his hand like King Canute stopping the tide.

"Enough," he said. "That's neither here nor there. The question is what to do about this Claude fellow."

"You're going to save him, aren't you?" Julie asked. She knew who he was, of course.

"That's in God's hands," Brother Luis replied. "I'll counsel him, of course, and prepare him to meet his maker. That's all a man of the Church can do."

Full of shit he was, and we were supposed to nod and look serious, but that was the point, I assumed. If he wanted to play, then — if only for Claude's sake — we would have to play too, hoping that eventually the rules of the game would become clear.

The wrinkle, of course, was that while most of us knew perfectly well that this monk was an arrant impostor, Isabel hadn't caught on. She'd been in Santa Fe for some time, and maybe she just didn't recognize him. Or maybe this church thing had begun to affect her mind so that she was taken in by the costume.

Obviously the Duke was getting off on this. We were his

audience and also his unwilling co-conspirators, because anybody who ruined the gag would have to answer eventually for what he or she had done, and none of us wanted to. There was, down the street, a real enough gallows and the enormous shadow it cast across the main street in the late afternoon.

Brother Luis announced that he was going down to the jailhouse to pay a call on poor Claude and give him what consolation the Scriptures offered. But before he did this, he wanted to know what Claude's chances were. Had Isabel talked with Angel? Had she asked him to spare her brother's life?

At a corner table in the Black Garter, Isabel told the monk her sad story — how Angel had offered her a deal whereby she could save her brother's ass if she were willing to offer a piece of her own.

"And you refused?" he asked.

"Of course," she insisted with some heat.

"Ah, excellent. A correct, a devout, an admirable answer."

"What else could I have said?"

He grinned. We could see in the shadow of his huge cowl the shine of his teeth, like the wolf's in Little Red Riding Hood. "You could have agreed."

"Never!"

"Oh, I don't mean that you would have done it. But if you were to have promised to meet him at night, in the dark, out behind the bar maybe . . . And if you sent some other woman in your place. . . "

"What other woman?"

"Any," I offered, having sat at a table nearby, where I could hear what they were saying. I saw how elegant it all was.

"Julie could go, which she would surely be willing to do to save Claude. She isn't planning to become a nun, after all. She might have a different view of what she is and isn't willing to do to save your brother. Or one of the girls who used to be down at Marianne's place, if you could find any of them."

"Or you could simply claim to have found one!" Brother Luis said, softly but with all the more authority.

"What?" Isabel asked.

I was puzzled myself there for a moment or two, until the good monk explained himself. "What it does, my child, is make the question easier. Or perhaps more difficult. It separates out what you actually do and what you are believed to have done. You could go to him and then later deny that it was you. No one would know. Your reputation would be, as your outer habit, spotless and immaculate. The actual condition of your underwear would be a private matter, something that only you and God would know about."

"That's the most disgusting idea I've ever heard in my life," Isabel said.

"I'm sorry. I was only trying to be helpful," Brother Luis said, and he took off for the jail and the fun of preparing Claude to face his imminent death, confessing sins that Luis — or the Duke — hoped would be original enough or at least numerous enough to be entertaining.

Not a bad fellow, after all, I thought. My kind of guy, in fact.

But why was he doing all this? Just out of boredom? That wasn't enough. He'd set all this complicated machinery into motion so that Isabel, the nun, would get laid. By Angel? What sense did that make?

Unless Isabel, pretending to be Julie or any other female in the territory, went to get laid by Angel, and out there in the hay wagon she met the Duke, who was standing in for Angel.

Standing in, or lying down.

IV

WHAT YOU HAVE TO UNDERSTAND is that there wasn't a whole lot to do in the Old West. I mean, before the trains came through, there wasn't even anything to read. There certainly wasn't anybody to talk to whose answers you couldn't predict. All there was out there was the desert, and you could go out and maybe watch one of those century plants and wait to see if it bloomed before you dropped dead. Or you could get drunk, or go down to Marianne's, or, if you were broke, just jerk yourself off.

I mean, it wasn't just a question of those wide open spaces between you and the horizon. Just as impressive and oppressive were those huge stretches of time between sunup and noon, and then even greater distances between noon and sundown, and sundown and sleep. Now and then you'd get a guy like the Duke who tried to occupy himself by thinking, which most people aren't any good at. And those who are? They find, as often as not, that it can be as much a danger as any other solitary vice.

Or that may just be my own hang-up because, as you've probably figured out already, that's my weakness too. And I must accuse myself along with the Duke, because I have the intellectual's inevitable sense of inadequacy, which is what you feel when you get to the point where you can figure out things but notice that your predictions are mostly wrong. Or, even worse, that what was right yesterday is wrong today. In short, that there's just no sense in anything, and that intelligence itself is a snare and a delusion, a kind of infernal joke.

Let's put the most generous construction on the Duke's first decision, however peculiar that may have been. Let's say that he really wanted to clean up Hotdog and establish a decent and civil town. But then Angel turns out to be corrupt, which has to be a disappointment. And the Duke realizes that he is not uncorrupt himself . . . ?

At what point does the Duke begin to wonder whether he's the prankster or the butt of the joke? And then, to avoid the necessity of consigning himself to the latter category, does he persuade himself that, all along, it was no more than a theatrical gesture? And to lend some support to that fragile intellectual construction, does he devise an entire system of impostures? If nothing is what it seems, then the Duke is not a dope, and Hotdog is no more than a fiction, one more mirage in the desert sunlight.

What I'm getting at is this: although Angel wanted to fuck the nun, the Duke may not even have been prompted by any desire for the girl. It was the intricacy, the sheer complication he loved, the notion that everyone was a token, a stand-in, a replaceable counter in some solitaire game.

Most guys, I'm told, think about sex forty or fifty times an hour. Now and then, a fellow conceives a passion for some particular piece of fluff and the frequency goes up to maybe fifty times a minute. But the Duke, I imagine, may have been beyond pussy-struck and, in a philosophical and dramaturgical fit, become altogether possessed. His possession expressed itself as sexual, but that could have been because we have only a pathetically narrow range of media in which to paint our landscapes and portraits.

Far-fetched, you say? (And I agree.) Nevertheless, you must remember that there was all this empty time and space out here in the West, with all this opportunity for refinement,

further elaboration, and then, in the end, brilliant simpli-
fication.

The hardest thing we learn, as little babies, is where we
stop and the world begins. It's what we're supposed to figure out at our mother's breast, right? That she is another, and
that you have to cry out to get her to come pick you up, put
the teat in your mouth, and give you suck. It's a hard lesson,
and not all of us master it. It's as if you have to compensate,
as if your mother having given birth to you, you now have
to give birth to her and to all the rest of the otherness out
there. Some of us have real trouble with that. And the curious truth is that it's the smartest of us who seem to have the
toughest time.

So there the Duke was, having seen Claude's pretty
sister. He could have been smitten — as Dante was smitten
by Beatrice, or Romeo by Juliet — so that the world changed,
collapsed, turned into a dreamscape in which each modest
and everyday object started to shimmer with grace or menace.
Or he could have been enchanted by his own momentary
ability to assign parts to the people around him, as if they
were figures in his fantasy life. Angel wants to put it to this
nice young lady? Nah, that's disgusting. Let him go fuck
chickens. The Duke will, pardon the expression, stand in for
him.

Nothing was neutral and merely itself in this new and
partisan universe. Anyone who was not a help to him was a
hindrance, and anything might be an omen. He began to persuade himself that he had worked out this bizarre business
with Claude and Angel and the gallows as just a way of getting Isabel back from the nunnery in Santa Fe . . . And the
dismaying bargain that Angel offered her? The Duke had ex-

pected that, was relying on it. That too was a part of the script.

But this doesn't mean that the Duke was happy. He would have felt a certain giddiness, because here he was exercising control over the whole town, but he was as much in play as anyone. His own actions surprised him. He was experiencing the trauma of all intellectuals when they find out that they can't even predict how they will behave themselves. That it isn't thoughts but actions that distinguish us, good from bad, brave from cowardly, important from trivial . . .

So how does he justify himself to himself? He tells himself yet another whopper — that it will all work out in the end. That there will be, in Hotdog, a new community, a decent place in which to live and work and play and bring up one's children. That part of it is how he's going to redeem himself and his town both! It's the novelist's cheat-sheet: knowing where he wants his story to end up. All he has to do is persuade his characters somehow to go along.

I confess I hadn't the vaguest idea that he had ventured so far into the realm of delusions as I watched him go down to the hoosegow to talk to Claude. But I figured that I'd mosey on down there with him. Why? Well, as I've suggested, there wasn't a whole lot else to do in Hotdog, and this was . . . interesting. But it was also true that I was pleased with myself for having figured out that this was, to some degree, a charade, a performance, and it struck me that no performance is complete without an audience. In order for a drama to resonate, there have to be spectators that hang on each word and gesture, appreciating the cleverness of the conception and recognizing the artistry and intricacy of the performances. And I guess I was also thinking that, if the Duke was

the main man in town, then it was likely that I might benefit from this special relationship with him. This connection,
after the performance was concluded, could be a convenient
thing.

What surprised me was that Claude went along with the
pretense that the man who had come to talk with him was
some kind of cleric. He must have recognized the Duke, but
he never let on. He played the whole scene, pretended to be
frightened of dying, and asked Brother Luis for comfort, courage, and faith. I guess he figured that if the Duke was the man
who could save him, he didn't want to risk causing him the
slightest degree of displeasure.

But would it have been displeasing? If I were doing some
bizarre thing like that, I'd surely want some reaction, some
degree of outrage . . . "You're doing this to me just so you
can fuck my sister, you low-down son-of-a-bitch!" would have
been the first words out of my mouth had I been Claude.

Maybe he had a different idea of theater. Or maybe he
was just a coward, and had been looking at that gallows long
enough so that he figured the safe thing was to play from
whatever cues the Duke gave him. In which case, the scene
was one in which he had to pretend to be a penitent, a poor
sinner, afraid not so much of death as of the judgment of our
Maker. Which he did pretty well, I must say. I sat down on a
box outside the jailhouse, got out a stick, and started to
whittle — this is something they actually do out west, as if
it were continually amazing that a steel knife blade can cut
wood. But what they're mostly doing is scheming, dreaming,
or eavesdropping . . . which, at the jail, wasn't at all difficult
to do. There were two windows, one in the office, and the
other — the one with the bars, of course — in the cell. It was

underneath that one that I'd arranged myself so I could listen to this serene nonsense.

"'I am the word and the light and the way and the path and the hope of the world,' saith the Lord. It is a vale of tears through which we walk, my son," Brother Luis intoned, "and though many are called and few are chosen, we all come at last to the same day of reckoning. My cup runneth over and mine enemies cry 'Ha ha!' But my God will protect me. A sincere penitent spirit is more precious than rubies and will win you your crown among the angels, just as your faith in the Lord will sustain you now in your time of trial."

"I do get a trial, don't I?" Claude said, prompted by the friar's momentary reference to recognizable reality. Claude couldn't have had much hope in due process, but he must have figured that it would at least take a little time. There might even be a jury, and . . . well, as Brother Luis might have put it, any straw looks good to the needle-eye of a rich drowning camel with a broken back.

The pious Brother didn't seem to have much confidence in the judiciary of Hotdog, however. "The justice of this world is not the justice of the Lord," he said. "My advice to you is to prepare your spirit."

"Thank you," Claude said with as much fervent humility as he could muster.

Astonishing! I could scarcely believe what I was hearing. But whether Claude understood where it was going or not, he couldn't have supposed that the prank would really go all the way to the gallows. Or, if it did, that there wouldn't be some dopey last-minute reprieve. Or a stagy rescue with a mounted band of masked men thundering down the main street of the town with guns blazing!

Those few of us who ever read anything knew the same dumb pulp fiction they were poring over back East. Unlike our eastern cousins, however, we had the choice of believing what we read or what we saw with our own eyes as we staggered and lurched through our mostly boring and strenuous lives — and, of course, we believed the books and the magazines!

I got up and went back to Julie's to have a cup of coffee, and I interrupted the two women there having another one of those dream scenes. Together they were playing out the Duke's demented script — without his even being there. They were, of course, chewing over the problem of whether or not Isabel would go and get herself stuffed — as she dearly wanted to do — at no risk whatever to her reputation.

A hell of a tough decision!

V

RAPE BY DECEPTION? It's one of the oldest plots in the world, even though — or because? — it shouldn't work. It's an implausible idea on its face and every other part of its body. The dream, though, is understandable — that we can play Zeus impersonating Amphitryon in bed. As someone else, we can get nookie and not be held responsible, not be . . . blamed for it. And if the world doesn't blame us, then maybe we don't have to blame ourselves.

But blame isn't really the problem so much as the griefs of the flesh, the indignities, the dreadful business of having to stop what you're doing in order to spend important time and energy running dumb errands for the body . . . that's what's intolerable. Have you never resented the time it takes to sneeze? You're reading, even reading this book, and you are (I flatter myself, perhaps, but we've come a good way) interested. But then your nose starts to tickle. You know that you can put it off for a while, maybe get to the end of the paragraph, but it tickles just enough to be distracting. You are going to sneeze, sooner or later, but if you breathe through your mouth maybe you can delay it, which you want to do because, let's face it, you've sneezed before. It is not entertaining. It turns you into an autonomic organism, reduces you a good many rungs down the great chain of being, so that you are occupied as intensely and as stupidly as your cat. Sneezing. Shitting. Peeing. Fucking. It's all a humiliation, one way or another. A distraction and an affront.

How nice, then, to avoid and evade the distress of it by playing a role and acting out, blaming another person for those proclivities you don't like to admit you have, even to yourself — sucking ear lobes, say, or having your hair pulled. It's an idea, then, that you see in plays and novels fairly often, but it doesn't work. I mean, get real! You know your wife pretty well. In the dark, you know what she smells like, what her heft is, what her preferences are. As she knows you.

Okay, but those two had never done it before. They were new to each other. Wouldn't that help? A little, maybe, but still not enough to convince me. The great thing about this plan — and I'm giving the Duke some credit here, because I think he deserves it — is that he had it set up so that each of the parties was pretending to be someone else. There was imposture on both sides, which meant that each one was distracted, restrained, entranced by this role-playing, and therefore less likely to be suspicious about the other.

I can imagine him imagining it. The truth is that we're all liars, that everyone makes love to a figment, and it isn't even a figment of the other person, but a projection of what that person might be thinking about you! A complicated transaction, but when a man's main squeeze is one of Marianne's girls, there's a lot of incentive for delusion. And to be disabused is to be driven to self-abuse.

The situation was as appealing as Isabel was, and certainly much more unusual. In any event, the Duke could figure that she would be preoccupied, not too particular about her partner, and also inexperienced.

Given enough time and interest, I might have guessed, but it would have been no more than pure conjecture, that in the next piece of business Angel, who was taking orders from the Duke, could claim to have been assaulted on the

way to the rendez-vous, cold-cocked as it were and left un-
conscious by some interloper.

In which case, his story would now be that A) he hadn't
nailed the nun, B) he had no idea who the son-of-a-bitch was
who'd decked him and fucked her, and C) he was more
determined than ever to hang poor old Claude, because . . .
because that was the least he owed himself, and for the sake
of honor.

The thing of it is that the Duke wanted more than just
this piece of Isabel's ass. He wanted to . . . to win her, to come
in like young Lochinvar to save her brother, redeem her reputation, put every wrong right, and make the whole damn
town look like the end of some old-timey comedy, with three
or four different couples who have been chasing each other
around in the woods getting sorted out in the right configu-
ration and, just before the curtain descends, happily married.

And who won't drink to that?

(You see? It would even be great for business down at
the Black Garter.)

He wanted Isabel, sure, but he wanted her because she
was there. She was available to play in his comedy. What he
really desired, I think, was to impose his will on our empty
landscape, to make the little dolls that kept crossing his line
of vision shape up and behave. A taste of power is a mighty
aphrodisiac. He was sick and tired of having us bobbing about
like random bubbles coming up from the bottom of a beer
glass. What he wanted — as which of us does not? — was
order, reason, shapeliness, harmony, logic. Above all, logic. His
own logic. He wanted to do *this*, and then watch as, inevitably, the result was *that*, and then the next thing, and then the
next. He wanted to turn his thoughts from the intellectual,
retrospective mode, which is passive and powerless, into the

prospective mode, so that he was not only predicting but actually creating the future.

So the big tryst, and then the bigger surprise, by which he could dazzle not only Isabel but every damned one of us.

This is my guess now, but what I did then was remind him that he was only a human being like any other, mere flesh and blood, and that what came out of his mouth was the same spit and hot air that any of us were capable of.

* * *

Next morning, Isabel was radiant. Fulfilled. Her destiny as a woman was for her to have this amazing and wonderful thing happen, and she had done it not for the fun of it but to prevent an injustice, sacrificing her fair white bod on behalf of her poor and reasonably innocent brother. Her cause had been the cause of heaven itself, and we were all to appreciate her sacrifice, to admire her selflessness, and to acknowledge the beauty and goodness of her altruism. Not even for a moment were we to allow ourselves to wonder whether she hadn't had a great old time for herself by the bye.

Okay, but if the Duke had left it there, how was he to come in looking like the hero he wanted to be? That was the intricate part of the plan, this new and desperate improvisation. The idea now was that Angel could announce he'd been knocked out the night before, that he hadn't been the one who got laid, that he was sore as hell, and that he was going to hang Claude that very day. No more farting around!

As you might expect, Isabel was appalled. She had her story about having arranged a stand-in, but what good was it if she knew that she'd been screwed and that it wasn't Angel who'd done it then but rather Angel who was doing it now, since the deal was off?

The good monk, sympathetic as he could be, had all the usual consoling things to say — about how God's justice is unerring while man's sublunary judgment is unreliable and often false. One must trust in the Lord! Oh yeah! All the usual bull-shit.

"We can't let this happen," I said to him quietly, meaning of course that *he* shouldn't. "We've got to stop it!"

"I am only a man of the cloth, an itinerant pilgrim, a voice crying out in the desert . . . " he said.

"Right! Sure! You're a vicious, manipulative, mean, lying son-of-a-bitch, and I swear, if you let Claude swing, I'll kill you, you understand me?"

Why did I do this? It purely beats the shit out of me. I am altogether at a loss. I learned what the Duke was trying still to deny — that we have no control over our own behavior. That we are what we act out. My acting out did not please him, however.

"Go fuck yourself," he quipped. "Keep your mouth shut or you're a dead man, and when I say it, it's not a piece of extravagant rhetoric or an empty threat. Claude will be okay, I tell you. But if you don't keep your trap shut, you won't be. You get me?"

So out we all go, the Duke, and Isabel, and Julie, and Angel, and Sophocles and the whole damn town, to watch the hanging. Which I now knew was rigged, a mere piece of theater, but which still looked pretty damned convincing, I must say.

Out Claude comes from the jailhouse with the black bag already over his head, and . . . and Gaspard is the hangman!

What the hell is this? A perfectly nice fellow, a minor clown, one of the guys who hangs out at the Black Garter, and he's the one who actually has to do the dirty deed? The murder — which is, let's face it, what's happening here — is turned over to some poor son-of-a-bitch who is too scared to refuse. And for the rest of his life, he's got to live with it. For no reason except his name happened to float across the Duke's consciousness at the wrong moment, he is changed from trivial bit-player to minor villain, and there is nothing he can do about it.

It scared the shit out of me, I'll tell you, because we are most of us vulnerable, as Gaspard was, to this kind of abrupt chasm opening up in the ground. And at the nutty whim of someone else, we can be turned into monsters, every man Jack of us. There's no sense in being proud of the fact that it hasn't happened to you yet. All that means is that the occasion has not yet arisen. But it could be lurking, waiting to spring at you . . .

I felt sorry for Claude, sure, but I felt real grief for Gaspard. And for myself, and for us all. The poor dope. I watch as he leads his victim up the steps and drapes the noose around his neck. And I am still thinking, okay, okay, it looks quite persuasive. What is the Duke going to do now, and how is it going to play out . . .

Then the trap springs, and the body falls, and the rope stretches . . . and the guy's fucking dead!

*   *   *

At this point it was too late to protest and altogether useless to accuse Brother Luis or the Duke or whatever he wanted us to call him. What would have been the good of saying, "Hey, you lied to us. You cheated. Make it good. Bring poor Claude back to life . . . "

Still, there was the purely academic question of what went wrong. I could see the general drift of what he was doing, could understand his bizarre motives, but for the life of me I just couldn't make any sense of this move, couldn't see how it would get him Isabel's gratitude, or respect, or love, or anything but undying enmity.

And it was purely to answer that question that had been going around in my mind that I found an occasion to ask him, later that day, just what the fuck he thought he was doing.

Or, no, not purely. Nothing in this world is pure. I wanted to confront him, I wanted to remind him that I knew what a swine he'd been. Or bumbler. Either way, if he was going to play God with other people's lives and deaths, he was, by God, responsible. I wanted him to look me in the face.

That's the real torment, I expect, in hell. The flames and sulfur and all that dopey stage-dressing are just ways of suggesting the agony it will be for us to have been understood, to have been judged by the omniscient God, and found every bit as woeful and inadequate as we have suspected all along in our worst but truest moments.

"So? What's the big surprise ending? What's the Duke got planned for us now?" I asked, ignoring the ridiculous clerical habit. We were out in back of the livery stable, not far from where he'd nailed Isabel before he'd killed her brother.

"So?" he asked.

"So? He's dead, you prick."

"Yes, he's dead. Dead as a post," he said. "But who is *he*?"
And then he laughed.

What was funny? It took me a moment.

"It wasn't Claude?" I asked.

"Nah, just some greaser horse-thief we were going to
hang anyway. I just kept him around a while until the right
moment presented itself. Wasn't it just swell!"

"Oh sure," I said. "Swell." And then, after a breath or
two, "You mean, Claude's all right?"

"Claude's fine. He's in a hell of a lot better shape than
you'll be if you breathe a word of this and spoil my fun. You
understand me?"

"I don't begin to understand you," I said. "But I take your
point."

"That'll do just fine," he said.

*   *   *

You see it, don't you? The nutty idea of substituting one body
for another in back of the livery stable led inevitably to the
only slightly nuttier idea of substituting one body for another
on the gallows. Sex and death are two sides of the same coin,
aren't they, and if a body is a body, then it really doesn't make
a whole lot of difference about whether it is jiggling down
there on the hay or up there on the gallows. Each of us has a
certain attachment to his own body, but that's just a matter
of habit, a sentimental indulgence. If the Duke was playing
God, then it was part of his theological experimentation to
assume that we were all identical units. A pawn is a pawn,
and you don't hesitate about the moral propriety of sacrificing one for the benefit of the other pieces. Only the player
is real — and the Duke was it.

Not that it's different back East. The trick there is that they cover it over, disguise what they're doing, so as to keep the rabble ignorant enough or drunk enough so that they think they're happy and don't revolt, turning as human chess pieces sometimes will to attack and destroy the ruthless sons-of-bitches who have been pushing them this way and that for reasons that have nothing whatever to do with their interests, preferences, or rights.

A bad business? Yes, it always is, but it was less bad, I had to admit, than what I'd supposed, because Claude wasn't dead. And it was only a matter of time before Brother Luis would uncowl himself, and the Duke would reappear to re-establish order, reason, calme, luxe, and volupté in Hotdog. And marry Isabel no doubt.

I mean, it looked like he'd bring it off after all!

VI

BIG FINISH! It's the convention, is it not? The poets legislate what we do, shaping our expectations, our very perceptions of external reality, in that we are uneasy unless the lives we lead conform to their conceits. A stage full of corpses. Or an elaborate minuet in which all the couples are united in matrimony. Or, in some of the more mannerist productions, a combination of these gestures, so that the corpses get up off the floor to take the hands of their appropriate mates and, with the other couples, form an attractively symmetrical pattern that may stand for the restoration of social order, the harmony of the spheres, or merely the willful conspiracy of the playwright and the audience.

It's too silly, of course, but we do it anyway, and even feel an inevitability in what we do. The Duke had it worked out so that we would all converge at this point, recognizing the rightness of the dispositions he had contrived for us, and assent . . . as some of us may, at last, assent, before we die, in the portion that God, Himself, has meted out for us.

"Portion?" "Meted Out?" What bizarre words they are, and how absurdly pretentious, but there is no other way to get close to what I assume the Duke was up to. His ambition was to mete out portions — of small potatoes, I am tempted to say, but his grandiloquence, I am afraid, was impervious to the wisecracks of supernumeraries like myself.

I can't even say that I blame him, particularly. It is just as likely the landscape that was at fault, that vastness waiting to be imposed upon or, even more provocatively, daring us to assert ourselves. The choice is always before us, I expect, between a passive acceptance of our place in nature, the quietist idea of being at one with the sagebrush, the mesas, and the sky, or, on the other hand, an active imposition of our intelligence, taste, judgment, and will.

Brother Luis went away, a mile or two down the road maybe, and then the Duke came back.

The performance could now conclude, as each of us said and did exactly what the Duke had contrived for us. Isabel complained to him about Angel and what a hypocrite he was, and a murderer, and, worse than that, a liar and a cheat. Because Angel's story is that he was hit on the head by somebody else . . . But how far can she go with her complaint if she isn't quite ready to admit that she was the one out there in the haystack?

Well, somebody went to get laid, and somebody laid her.

And for that, brother Claude ought to have been let off the hook and, more to the point, the noose below it, to which he had been so unfairly condemned (for fornication yet). And here the Duke was, playing out his little charade with more flourishes than the occasion perhaps warranted. He concurred in Claude's sentence, agreed that he'd been a bad boy and, while he regretted the death of any citizen of Hotdog, it was a question of public morals and the survival of the whole town . . .

An invitation, wouldn't you say, to some irreverent comment? At the very least a few ripe raspberries to garnish this grand compote?

"It was Brother Luis," I said. "He was the one who was messing in our affairs, undertaking all these assignations and substitutions. And he wasn't even a real cleric, I'd bet my burro, but a pretender, a rank impostor, and a clown!"

"How so?" the Duke asked.

"The brother spoke most unflatteringly of you, sir," I told him. "A great whoremaster and waterer of drinks, he called you. And a pompous ass. And a needledick. And many other even less flattering appellations and cognomens."

"That'll be enough of that," he said.

Which only made it more fun. I was getting to him a little? "If it wasn't Angel out there, making the old jig-a-jig, then I'll bet it was fat-assed Brother Luis, huffing and puffing over whoever it was that Isabel sent in her place."

"Shut the fuck up," he said.

I bowed low as if to celebrate what was clearly my victory, and from then on kept quiet.

More witnesses and complainants, and counter-complainants, and then the *coup de théâtre* when old Gaspard showed up to ask forgiveness for having screwed up. He admitted that he'd gone and hanged, inadvertently, the wrong man. Hanged the wrong man? Oh no! How could it be? And then we realize that Claude is not, after all, dead and buried, but quick and alive and full of beans. Ta-DA!

Julie is beside herself with joy. Isabel is delighted. And grateful. So much so that she accepts forthwith the Duke's proposal of marriage. Except that. . .

Blushes, shy looks, and then whisper whisper . . .

She confesses to him, being fundamentally a good girl, that she is no longer a virgin.

Grins from the Duke. And then, "Yes, I know," by which he means to let her know that he was the guy on the hayrick and that all this extravagant foolery has been for her sake, a way of saving her from herself and her damnfool notion of hiding herself away in that convent in Santa Fe.

She is grateful for that, too. And so now there can be

two weddings, the Duke and Isabel's, and Julie and Claude's.

Or three, because the stagecraft demands it. Marianne, the old madame, without whose collusion none of this nonsense could have been managed, reappears, and she is to marry . . . Me?

Evidently. It's my punishment, or my reward, or say, with less english on the English, fate. Promiscuity and the swapping of sex for money were what I was running away from, and therefore running toward.

Even though the Duke didn't know any of this when he worked it out. The idea just occurred to him.

"Why?" I asked him. "What's the point? Why do you need this?"

"I don't need it," he told me. "But it pleases me. The neatness of it. Besides, you're the wild card, the only one who understands what has been going on. Which means, I can't have you around here unpunished. You want to leave? You can do that. But if you stay, you marry Marianne, just so you won't be able to put on airs and act . . . superior to any of the rest of us."

"Superior? Or equal?" I asked him.

"That's just what I'm talking about. In the Old West, I'd have shot you dead in the street, and no one would have complained. But we're town folks now. And you're either going to make an honest woman of Marianne or get out of Hotdog. You got that?"

I nodded.

"Okay then. Pour yourself a drink," he said. "On me. To celebrate the happy ending. I just love happy endings, don't you?"

Lorenzo's Book

I

HOW IS THE DOUBLE MAN TO BE TRUE TO HIMSELF? All our ideas of loyalty assume a singularity of heart and mind I can imagine as the attributes of angels in their rapture — and of devils in their enraged torment — but not of human beings, imperfectly modeled, mottled (even motley) as we all are and full of our contradictions. The only true man, then, is the double agent, true to his doubleness, to the contradictoriness of his impulses and his affections, his alternating moods and humors. He does not spy for the money, does not labor for the gold, but loves the guilt, the notion that he is at any moment betraying something dear to him by serving something else that is no more dear *sub specie aeternitatis* but only for the moment available, attractive, or convenient. So some lovers enjoy most to lie down with a woman and imagine her reproaches, her pain, her complaint on that very day when she shall be left alone and the man gone to some other bed, in which another *bella donna* waits, thinking — the fellow thinks — of him. Intricacy, intractable intricacy. They call it baroque, but it is a kind of simple truth, obvious and blunt as a straight line in a painting where there is no other straight line. Our souls are crooked, full of crazy scrollwork and embellishment, draped, etched, and chiseled . . .

I am Lorenzo. If any eyes ever scan these pages, it is a fair guess that the brain to which they connect will have stored away some information about me, most of it wrong. In the past few years, I have become a kind of folk hero (or, more accurately, a folk supporting-player) known for my goodness, my gentleness, my simplicity. It is all nonsense, or almost all. I was there in Verona. I played a part in the events that have been enacted upon the stages of the world, but in a transmogrified form I can only smile at. The requirements of the public are for abrupt reversals, the suffering of young lovers, the chagrin of age and authority, a liberal spicing up of the dish of experience the world serves us. The truth is an acquired taste, and if refined palates crave it, part of the reason, I think, is that, like the truffle of Périgord, it is a rare commodity. Indeed, one could maintain that too much of it will cause indigestion, convulsions, stupor, coma, and death — which makes it a poison, as the Church has always supposed (why else monitor the truth or try to control it — even to control the truth about the truth?).

But that is another subject for another volume. My concern here, having leisure in God's abundance and the inclination (or arrogance?), is to reclaim a little of my own history from the garble that has gone forth about me, and about us all. The features of Romeo and Giulietta have been obliterated like the faces on coins that have been too much handled, and in the absence of any distinguishable physiognomy they have been assigned the conventional masks of traditional lovers. It is important, therefore, to reassert some differentiation, to reach across the dull cartoons they have become to the people they actually were.

He was something of an oaf. And she was thirteen years old. Oh, they mention her age but then they ignore it. Convention takes over, inexorably, and she is merely nubile, indistinguishable from any young woman of any place and any time.

They also get Verona wrong. It is turned into a stage set with ramparts in the foreground of the drop cloths, and wooded hills beyond.

Let us recognize it as a typical town, but put it in Italy, in the backwaters of the Veneto. Let it be typically corrupt, typically venal, typically selfish and cruel — and then it begins to resemble the Verona I knew. I was sent there, after all, not as a reward for my outstanding services and conspicuous abilities, but as a punishment, as much deserved as any punishment ever is. One is punished for having been clumsy enough to get caught. But, again, that's a matter for another treatise.

The real place, then, was a small town with a quite impressive Roman amphitheater and a couple of decent churches, one of them with a remarkably fine rose window. A river. An assortment of predictable public buildings, shops, stables, palazzos and . . . what you'd expect to find anywhere. But on a small scale. Here, there were two leading families of what we have learned to call the middle class. The Scaliger princes were less powerful than they might otherwise have been, because of the proximity of Venice, which was, as has been said to the point of boredom, Queen of the Adriatic. Anything so frequently repeated is bound to be incorrect, and this sobriquet too is false. She was the Shopkeeper of the Adriatic. Which meant that the mercantile families in the Veneto had considerable power.

The Montecchi and the Capelletti were powerful enough, together, to outweigh the Prince of Verona. And the Prince, who was not a fool, must have understood these realities, and I always supposed that, in order to preserve his own authority, he was keeping the two leading mercantile families at odds. It stood to reason. Divide and conquer. He could never say he was doing this, never admit that it had even crossed his mind. But that was the obvious policy by which he could maintain his authority. On the other hand, in all his public utterances he had to declare that the quarrels of the Veronese were a wound in his side, were disgraceful, distressed him, that he wanted peace and harmony, that he deplored the fighting and wished to have tranquility and understanding. And so on, and so forth. Real harmony would have meant the end of Scaliger authority, and he knew that, but like many public men he began after a time to believe in what he was saying.

The Montecchi and the Capelletti assumed that the maundering pronouncements the Prince made on ceremonial occasions were to be taken with more than a grain of salt. I supposed them to be — like the flags and bunting and the uniforms on the cowardly guards — conventional decoration for these occasions, trotted out, displayed, and then put away until next time. One person, however, seemed to give credence to every word the man spoke. She was quite alone in this belief, but the saying is that love is blind. I remember how shocked — not to say distressed — I was upon discovering her in the confessional one day.

"Father?" she asked. It is not an implausible way to begin. I assumed that the confessor was making sure that there was someone on the other side of the grillwork.

"Yes, my child?"

"Father!"

"Yes?"

"What on earth are you doing here, Father?"

"I don't understand," I said. And I didn't. And it took

some time before I realized that her mode of address was biological and not just ecclesiastically appropriate. "Rosaline?"

"Yes, Father."

"What are you doing here?" I asked.

She laughed — which is irregular in a confessional — and informed me that she had been living in Verona for some years. I was the newcomer. I was the intruder, she meant, although she did not go quite so far as actually to say so. Recognizing her exercise of restraint, I suggested that we repair to the rectory for some wine and conversation. Conversation in a confessional is . . . awkward. One can't look into the other person's face.

She had much to tell me, and with great volubility she informed me of the progress she had made, the great difficulties she had overcome, the hopes she entertained. God! It was all very self-congratulatory and, at least by implication, critical of me for not having provided her with the advantages to match her lofty opinion of her true worth. And yet, to be fair, she had done well enough. And to rise in the world one needs an exaggerated opinion of one's merits. That way, the struggle to improve one's station is not merely ambition but a more general putting the world's affairs in order, an effort in the direction of justice and the harmony of things.

Perhaps not. Nevertheless, there was an impressive fervor in her exertions over the course of the five or six years since I'd last seen her. She had managed to pass herself off as the illegitimate daughter of the late Doge of Venice, which enabled her to skulk along the chair railings of rather grander salons than those to which she was entitled as my illegitimate daughter. Our connections are . . . respectable. An uncle of mine was a general in the armies of Lucca — famous in his day for negotiating favorable conditions for surrender. And a great-aunt of mine was once mistress to a pope — or claimed to have been. He died before proper provision could be made for her (and therefore for all of us). The mention of her name was helpful in getting me admitted to the seminary, but as for tangible rewards, we have been left to seek them for ourselves.

My daughter, Rosaline, had been seeking fairly assiduously, I must say. Having given herself airs — or at least forebears — she had managed to insinuate herself into the very highest circles, having become more or less mistress to the Prince of Verona.

"And I mean to consolidate that position," she insisted.

What she meant was that she intended for him to marry her.

"Unrealistic," I warned her. "And unlikely. Because he has more power as a bachelor than he could possibly have as a married man."

I, who had been in Verona only a very short time, a little less than a month, had to explain to her how the Prince could hold open the possibility of an alliance with either house — with the Capelletti or with the Montecchi, playing their ambitions and their envies and enmities as carefully as a musician plays the different stops of an organ with the different keyboards and the pedals.

Rosaline, however, was interested not at all in my music lessons or my metaphors. She was altogether single-minded, as the ambitious frequently seem to be. Toward her objective she ran like a blindered horse.

If I had been aware of the consequences of such unswerving dedication to her goal of personal aggrandizement, I expect I should have been willing to do my duty as a citizen of Verona, as a member of the clergy, as the Prince's spiritual advisor, and as a father, too. I could have exposed her, told the Prince that she was not the Doge's daughter, and conducted her to a convent, where she would be out of harm's way. But I didn't. We all are subject to occasional fits of sentiment, are we not? I confess that I was moved by the brusqueness of her conversation, her lack of any respect or affection for me, her selfishness and her pride — all of which proclaimed her as the daughter of my heart as well as of my loins. Besides, she was a very handsome young woman, striking, tall, almost severe looking, but with a prominence of lip and eye and bosom that can beguile. I wondered just how far she could go. And if she went as far as my imagination conducted her, then the information I possessed about her paternity might prove valuable.

I had no thought of blackmail, mind you. It was simply a provision I had to make for her observance of filial obligations. It is a commandment, is it not? The pressure one brings to bear on one's child in order to steer her toward the path of virtue . . . But I sound as if I am delivering a sermon, which is not my intention.

"How, then, do you propose to convince the Prince that he does not need to hold out the prospect of matrimony in order to manage the destinies of his city?"

"Not convince, Father. Demonstrate," she said, runically for effect.

"What, if anything, are you talking about?" I asked her. The best defense against the runic is the condescending.

"Of course, I understand that when the Prince makes speeches, he is only . . . making speeches. Or I hope that's the case. Nevertheless, if one were to take him at his word and accomplish what he claims to desire, then he'd have no possible grounds for objection, would he?"

I was, by this time, quite lost. And I told her so. "If there is a subject to this verbiage, I'd be deeply grateful to learn what it might be!"

"Peace. Peace in Verona. An end to the bickering between the Capelletti and the Montecchi. Harmony, tranquility, order."

"You sound like a religious enthusiast, which is, given my profession . . . in questionable taste."

"If I can arrange that peace in Verona he's always talking about, he'd have to marry me."

It was a curious proposition. So far as I could see, the conditional clause and the independent clause were only tenuously connected with one another.

"You must be a person of extremely good luck," I told her. "Why would he *have* to marry you?"

"He'd have no excuses left to remain single."

"Granted. And he'd perhaps consider marriage. But why would he consider marriage to *you*?"

"Because he is a good person. Because he'd be ashamed of himself if he tried simply to ditch me."

"That's the stupidest thing I've heard in all my life."

"Surely you exaggerate," she said. "But the obtuseness is his, not mine. I must be mindful of the nature of the man I'm trying to manipulate, mustn't I?"

How sorry I am, now, to admit that I looked at her with some approval. She was my progeny, not my protégée; still, one tends to confuse these roles. I offered her a little more of our local Valpolicella and inquired how she had managed to find her way to Verona in the first place. I had not seen her for some years, not since I had left the seminary in Ravenna, where Rosaline had been one of the young waifs in the orphanage. Her mother, the prettiest of the nuns, had de-

livered the girl one night with the help of some of her sisters
in Christ, had put the girl in a basket, had left the basket on
the doorstep of the orphanage, and — I should imagine within
a matter of seconds — found the basket she had left. Out of
a sense of self-preservation as much as anything, the nun kept
from the little Rosaline the identity of her ancestry and never
showed her any favoritism, but the child blossomed nevertheless, as she ought to have done, having me as a father and
the nun (a young woman of noble birth and real talents) as
a mother. It was with no great effort that Rosaline learned the
accomplishments required of young ladies — needlework,
singing, French, Latin, painting. All the fine and practical arts.
She had them and, at a fairly early age, a figure as well. So
she was hired as a governess by a count from Ravenna who
did not even wait to get home before taking her virginity —
in the coach!

It is a persistent assumption of our poets and playwrights
that a woman's first lover holds a special place in her affections forever, that the pattern of associations in the heart is
as automatic as that of the mind. And there may be some
truth to this. But in my daughter's case, it was an association
not so much with this particular count as with the coach, the
novelty of the world outside the orphanage, the brevity of
their acquaintance with one another. In short, she became
infatuated not so much with the count himself as with her
own sexuality and attractiveness, her own power. She came
to believe in the lightning flash and the thunderclap, in overwhelming and irresistible mutual attraction, in the impromptu coupling that she took as a tribute to her beauty. It was a
kind of fetishism, really, but not so crippling as most fetishes.
Indeed, hers was unusual because it gave her confidence and
courage — not to say brashness. Before a month had elapsed,

she had seduced the eldest son of the count, had elicited from that young infatuate an offer of marriage, had returned to the father to negotiate a settlement, had been bought off at a very impressive figure, and had left Ravenna for Venice, where she intended to establish herself, seek her fortune, and become one of the great ladies of the age.

Needless to say, she didn't quite make it. But she had her moments of success as well as failure. She confided to me that her chances would have been much better if there had been carriages in Venice. The motion of the gondola is too gentle, soporific rather than aphrodisiac, lulling rather than inspiriting. Furthermore, even a city like Venice is only so large, and the important people are few indeed. After a time, she had met most of them, knew which ones were celibate, or asexual, or homosexual, or in other ways malapropos. She believed, still, in the arrival of the mysterious stranger who would crush her to his chest, carry her away, and change everything.

But there were no strangers left. There were only tourists and businessmen and petty princelings of the surrounding towns in the Veneto — like our Prince, for instance. She saw him at a party, decided on very little evidence that he was, indeed, the one (I must suppose that she inquired and discovered him to be neither married nor homosexual) and followed him. Even to Verona!

Her stratagem for the contrivance of an introduction was boldly original. She sent him an invitation to a tryst — in the shadows of the amphitheater, which is a notorious place for ruffians and villains. He supposed — as she expected him to suppose — that this was a threat more than an invitation, that there would be an assassin rather than an adoring lady. He sent some thug, a bravo disguised as himself, in order to find out who was trying to kill him. Rosaline received the bravo, pretended not to know he was not the Prince, welcomed him into her carriage, and took him for a quick ride, depositing him back at the palace with a last twitch and kiss, so that the Prince learned — as she knew he would — how he had deceived himself.

The idea of what he had missed drove him crazy. And she did not do what he expected her to do, hoped she'd do, burned for her to do, as he waited day after day for that second invitation. She did nothing, leaving it to him to try to find her, the mysterious woman, the admirer, the succubus, the angel-whore . . . She left the construction of categories to the play of his fancy. It was impossible, of course, for the Prince to identify this passionate stranger. And the bravo's recollection was not of her face so much as other, less immediately visible attributes, impossible to ascertain on any wide-scale survey. She waited for him to despair of ever knowing for himself what this marvelous creature was like, and then, at a large reception honoring the grape harvest, she whispered in his ear that she missed him.

"Madame? Do we know one another?"

"Intimately," she said, still in a whisper but her eyes fluttering commandingly.

"I beg your pardon . . ." He broke off, having decided she had to be the one. "The amphitheater?"

"You remember?"

"Yes," he said. What else could he possibly say? He could not admit that one of his paid thugs had impersonated him, not if he ever hoped to see her again (for the first time).

"I had hoped to hear from you," she said.

"But how was I to find you?"

"I put that little paper into your hand, remember?"

"Paper?"

"Yes, with my name. My address."

Obviously the fool had lost it. It had fallen out of the carriage, or had crumbled to dust in his pocket, or been laundered into a sodden pulp. There were all sorts of plausible stories, had he needed to invent one. Or had she required one. But it was all beside the point. He had found her. He was delighted. The allure of a first rendezvous and the joys of a reunion, improbably combined as they were, approximated her own rather odd notions about the fateful brief encounter, at once casual and yet somehow connected to the inner workings of the greatness of the universe.

From this intricate beginning, what wonders ought to have followed? I have no idea what she expected, or what the Prince expected. But it would have been obvious to me that there would be a dreadful falling off, a descent into the banal. The two of them adored each other, delighted each other, and very shortly became domestic. He installed her as his more or less official mistress. She moved into the palace, retaining her own rooms in a nearby villa for the sake of propriety, and perhaps as a place to retreat to, should the need arise. Her imagination had exhausted itself, and all she could dream of now was to become his wife and the principessa of the Veronese.

"Not exactly a novel ambition, but sturdy. Solid. It has a nice gravitas," I told her.

"Thank you," she said, perhaps a little wryly, as if to let me know she did not give much of a damn whether I approved or not. "But as I say, it is necessary for me to establish, if only in a temporary way, at least the illusion of civil harmony in the city." The qualifications — temporary and illusion — betrayed some realistic thinking. Peace in Verona was an impossible project, but the temporary illusion of peace

— particularly where the signs of hostility were so extravagant and abundant — might actually be managed. It was theoretically possible, at any rate.

"And how do you expect to accomplish this minor miracle?" I asked her.

"With your help."

"Mine? Why mine?"

"Because you are my father."

"And as my daughter, as my own flesh and blood, you ought to have enough shrewdness not to presume too much upon that connection."

"And you are ambitious."

"None of us is immune altogether. What are you getting at?"

"This is not the kind of place you had hoped to end your days in, is it? A word from the Prince to Venice, and there could be a more appropriate use of your accomplishments in a more — how shall I say? — a more distinguished setting. It could be a very good thing for you. We could both benefit."

"I never trust cooperative ventures," I told her. "There is always a point where the mutuality of interest ends and different goals present themselves to the parties. And I never trust relatives."

"It is no great sacrifice I am asking you to make. It is a little thing, in fact."

"It always begins with a little thing. Then eventually, there is something just a little larger, a little more strenuous. Then the world."

"You can always change your mind."

"I don't have to change my mind, though, if I begin by refusing."

"You won't even hear what I have in mind?"

"I doubt that I can prevent your telling me."

"The Capelletti have a little girl, do they not?"

And so on.

The story is well enough known that I see no point in drawing out the process of discovery. What she had in mind was a match that she and I should engineer between the Monteccho boy and the little Capelletta. The nuptials would not only produce a temporary illusion of that harmony she required for her own purposes but would also set a kind of example, give just the right subconscious nudge to her somewhat slow-footed Prince. Finally, her aims having been accomplished and her dreams turned into vital statistics, she would see to it that the Church promoted me and transferred me to a more suitable and more cosmopolitan post. Venice? Florence? Bologna? Milan? Or even Rome? Why not?

A shapely fiction, but a fiction nevertheless. Indeed, the giveaway is its shapeliness. Nothing is that neat. In the real world, people refuse to behave like orderly characters. They balk, hesitate, vacillate, temporize, lurch forward and fall back in the most unpredictable ways. Still, a connection with the royal family, however impromptu, was not to be dismissed. More to the point, I was not at all sure I could afford, at this early stage in my Veronese career, to offend my daughter, whose power and prospects I could hardly gauge, and whose enmity, therefore, I did not at all desire. I agreed to look into it, at least to take that first step down the road. My intention was to go only far enough to gain her trust and then, at a fair and decent opportunity, betray her or threaten to — in order to get her to do what she should have done in the first place, which was to obey the commandment and offer unselfishly to make my life richer, fuller, easier, and more amusing.

It is a daughter's duty.

II

IN THE QUARREL BETWEEN the Capelletti and the Montecchi there were no issues involved; no principles of any kind were in question. Indeed, my impression was that the two houses would have agreed on practically all issues and questions, much as two lions roaming the same savannah, or two trees struggling for the same patch of sunlight would, in all likelihood, agree with one another on all principles and assumptions. The two of them were examples of natural forces, mindlessly accumulating capital and just as mindlessly talking about the public good, the common weal, the destiny of Verona . . . God knows what rot!

I sound — and am — contemptuous, but I am also honest enough to recognize that both the Prince and I were decorations, ornamental distractions to the reality that the Capelletti and the Montecchi embodied. They were Verona. We were vestiges of an earlier and a more decorous time, allowed to continue to mime our functions because it was convenient, even necessary, for the ambitions and the appetites of these mercantile organizations. They were disguised as families, but they were businesses from the patriarchs down to the swaddling babes. Bonds of affection there were none. Instead, flow charts dictated relationships. They did not marry; they merged. And they did not make love so much as they combined to produce branch managers and clerks.

And they spoke, not only to outsiders but to themselves as well, in the most lofty, pious, idealistic terms, which would put to shame any prince or cleric or cavalier.

It took me some time to draw these conclusions —
several visits at any rate. I had occasion to call upon them very
soon after arriving in Verona. I felt, in both households, a
peculiar discomfort, as if there were a joke I was not getting.
It first struck me that my apparent piety was the cause of this
barely restrained hilarity. I said some slightly less than pious
things, in order to put Capelletto at his ease, in order to let
him know I was an actual human being, a servant of the Lord
but not the Lord, Himself. Capelletto was shocked, disappointed, and somewhat hurt. I was supposed to be the pure
and simple priest, so that he could play at being the pure and
simple parishioner. If anyone saw through any of his impostures, then all of them might be revealed and the entire struc-
ture of his life might be brought down in a catastrophic
twinkling. The humor, then, was in the piety, in the joy with
which we played to each other's playing. Stepping out of
character would have been bad manners.

I disliked the fellow, of course, but not for himself so
much as for what he turned me into. I could see him dimin-
ishing me to that stick figure he required, a fugitive from
some children's pageant. (And inevitably, this is exactly what
I have been turned into — which ought to prove that
Capelletto is the new man, the emblem of the age, its prod-
uct, its producer, its destiny.)

The house was one of those urban fortresses with several
different tiers of columns on the facade, suggesting a series
of temples piled one on top of the other. In fact, that
suggestion was not inappropriate, for the air of the place was
worshipful, the self-regard of Capelletto having approached
the condition of mystical awe. Everything was too bright, too
neat, too shiny, too new. The decent feeling of having been
lived in that one enjoys in a house was not something

Capelletto experienced or even understood. He liked what was new, what was barely unwrapped from the shop, what had the look of having only recently had a price tag affixed with a little twist of string. The result was a peculiar aura of instability. The house felt as if everything one saw in it had been produced within the past half hour, had been assembled and displayed within the past five minutes — and might therefore be disassembled and removed at any time. And with Signora Capelletto's changing notions of what was fashion- able and desirable, rooms were as likely as not to be disas- sembled and redone between one's visit on Tuesday and one's next visit on Thursday. Lamps, tables, tapestries, statuary wandered around the rooms and transformed themselves in shape and color as if in obedience to mysterious natural laws.

Capelletto himself was a tall, muscular fellow who looked like a farmer, with hands like hams and great fleshy jowls hanging over a meaty neck of heroic proportions. He was self-conscious about his appearance, probably disliking it because of the way it revealed his peasant ancestry. That self- consciousness was rather engaging. It was the only relief in an otherwise dismal landscape of single-mindedness and smug satisfaction.

His wife was of a respectable family, her father being the younger son of a minor nobleman of Vicenza. She was small, rather delicate looking, and with a brightness of eye and a flightiness of attention that not only made me think of a bird but surprised me each time I saw her: how very birdlike, how extremely avian, I thought, struck anew each time. But if she was like a bird, it would have to be the magpie — for she shared with her husband a passion for objects.

I made their acquaintance, as I say, very soon after arriving in Verona, and found them to be useful members of the church, always ready to provide an altarcloth or a chalice, if only to match the generosity of the Monteccho household — as if the Church were a great auction house where salvation was for sale to the highest bidder.

I confess that I did not preach against this heresy or try to disabuse them — Montecchi or Capelletti — of their fancies. I assumed that the business of their just rewards or punishments would be seen to by a greater wisdom than my own. And the benefit was that of the church and not mine. I could afford, therefore, to be somewhat latitudinarian. Their motives — like their views about the possibility of the bodily assumption of the Virgin — were their own business.

What Rosaline wanted me to do was interview the Capelletto girl and discover her inclinations and prospects. Inasmuch as this was a very easy thing for me to arrange, I contrived a meeting. Or I went over there with that intention. In the event, I did not have to do any contriving whatsoever. They insisted that I meet with the girl, bringing it up themselves and asking me, as a favor, to have a talk with her.

"She is becoming difficult," Capelletto told me. "We have arranged a match for her, and she is reluctant."

"She dislikes the young man?"

"She has never laid eyes on him." Capelletto bellowed. "So there is nothing for her to dislike. She is merely being willful."

"Perhaps what she dislikes is the fact that she's never laid eyes on him."

"But he is a count," Capelletto told me.

I understood at once. What Capelletto was buying was a coat of arms. The Medici had a coat of arms; he needed one, too. His daughter, married to a count, would be entitled to arms — or a lozenge? (I would have to look this up.) It would put a seal of respectability upon his exertions in the arena of commerce.

I could hardly tell him what a coincidence it was that I should be asked to expound upon the commandment to honor one's parents, having had occasion to resort to it earlier that very day with my own daughter. Still, there was an effervescent pleasure in the suppression of this impulse to share a confidence. I looked as grave as I could manage — which is very grave, indeed! I have a knack for ecclesiastical solemnity, of which I am especially proud because it is a mood absolutely foreign to my character. Off I marched to see Giulietta, while Signor and Signora Capelletto wrung their hands in concern behind me.

Obviously, it was not uppermost in my mind to try very hard to persuade the girl to obey her parents and marry this count. That would have put an end immediately to my daughter's scheme — profiting neither her nor myself. I was intending to persuade badly, to advocate her parents' wishes ineptly, to provide just that kind of smarmy exhortation that produces — in anyone of taste and character, and in nearly all adolescents — an immediate and opposite impulse.

But then I stepped into the room, introduced myself to her formidable nurse, and was introduced in turn to the girl.

Small, like her mother. Delicate features, not so much miniature as precisely defined. A wonderful clarity to the eyelids, the flanges of the nostrils, the modeling of the lips, the line of the chin and the jaw, the angle of the neck. Not an immediately impressive beauty, but attractive, pleasant, and comely, inviting further scrutiny, further attention and even study. Only later on, after more scrupulous appraisal, did her qualities begin to reveal themselves: her delicacy, her ebullience, her gamine gaiety, which could abruptly subside to a heart-wrenching soulfulness.

But I get ahead of myself. I was taken with the girl, even at that first encounter, but not carried away, not bowled over. I think my first reaction was one of comprehension — how Capelletto had seen her as a piece of valuable goods, had made an advantageous bargain for her, as any merchant would try to do, and was understandably frustrated by her reluctance to go along with his arrangements. I understood that first of all, and the irony of such a delightful creature having been given to these parents. The world is improbably arranged so that even our good fortune tests us. On the other hand, she was too good for the Monteccho boy, too, as I was even then able to see.

There are, I suppose, explanations that could be offered. She was poised on the threshold of womanhood, a wonderful mixture of contrarieties, like a bird on a branch about to take flight, all the more still and full of repose because of its readiness to soar and swoop. That is too poetic. In a more practical way, she managed to appeal to me across a broad range of responses that most of us keep separate most of the time. Some women are maternal and some more or less daughterly, but she was both. Some women are rather spiritual and ethereal, and some more fleshly and sensual, but she was both.

I had a daughter, had just come from talking with Rosaline, and felt . . . less than at peace about her. I had missed most of her childhood, had been deprived of the opportunity to mold her into the young woman I wanted her to become. My failure was clear to me, and although it was not my fault, I blamed myself. We blame ourselves most when we have the least control over what has happened.

Here was the daughter I should have had. Even better, she could be a daughter who would not be forbidden me by the taboos of society and the Church. Fathers invest their efforts and emotions into the lives of daughters, and then what happens? They leave. They go off with some clown, some clod, some callow bumpkin who has no appreciation, no real discernment, nothing but youth and lust . . .

"You have been difficult," I said, but with an inflection that was not severe. It was not quite a question, not quite congratulatory, and not at all condemning. She looked up at me, tried to guess whether there was some kind of trap in my approach, considered the situation, and decided to try me. "Yes," she agreed brightly.

I stared at her. We stared at each other, in defiance but complicity, too. It was a kind of game.

"You have been having impure thoughts," I suggested.

"Me? Impure thoughts? No."

"None?"

"I don't think so."

"Not about the man your father wants you to marry," I admitted, "but about someone else?"

"Certainly not about him. I've seen a painting of him. He is not attractive."

"And therefore you have been imagining other men," I suggested. "But that is very wrong. You must fight against this. You must resist. You must think about not thinking about fornication."

"I should think that would be very difficult, if I were to try actually to do that."

I liked her a lot. The gaiety of the girl, the way she was able to show delight without giggling or blushing, but in a steady, straightforward, enthusiastic heartiness, appealed to

me. And it was no doubt a pleasant surprise for her that I was
not about to bully her by putting the voices of God and the
Church into a chorus behind her parents' shrill duet.

My intentions? It is difficult to remember now just what
they were at that early instant. I think I wanted to gain her
confidence, which I needed for the sake of Rosaline's scheme.
It is not unlikely that I was even then contemplating some
sort of benign mischief, the shape of which wasn't clear, but
which would have as its general purpose the frustration of
Capelletto's ambitions. I had no personal animosity toward
the fellow. Our differences were more profound — of style
and attitude. If he was living in the world correctly, then I was
a misfit, a sport, an aberration. And the reverse condition
produced, of necessity, the reverse conclusion — if I were
correct and in tune with the world's workings, then he was
anomalous and a freak, the sort of creature to arouse the
instant enmity of the rest of the flock, for the common good
and the survival of the species.

My guess, informed as it is by later events, would be that
I was the misfit — and that my gloom was the inevitable
consequence of my understanding that my peculiar kind was
doomed. It became all the more necessary, then, for me to
make my mark upon a world my kind was all but fated to
quit.

We joked and played for the better part of an hour,
Giulietta and I. It was my purpose at that first meeting to
establish a few lines of communication demonstrating that,
as ill-assorted as we seemed, we could amuse each other. This
demonstration required no effort at all on my part. Indeed, I
wondered afterwards whether she, for her own reasons, might
have been trying to beguile me. If so, we were both successful, and it was the most natural thing in the world for us both

to seek a way of continuing our entirely agreeable exchange of views. Her life was fairly rigidly circumscribed, but I had my church for us to hide in. No one could possibly object to my efforts to instill in her the great ideals and moral values of the Church. It was religious instruction. She got her release time.

But nothing is ever as simple as it appears. And we simplify as we remember, putting intentions where there may have been merely outcomes, and ignoring intentions that came to nothing. There was the nurse, whom I have almost forgotten. (Whom I should like to forget? Yes, that too.) Curiously, she has earned a place in the folk tale, an odd little niche wherein she is enshrined as a conventional grotesque, a role for young actresses to play, made up to look old and cackling like a Harpy. She was nothing at all like that. Prim, strident — repressed, I suppose — she was a deliberate choice by the Capelletti to guard Giulietta and yet to kindle in her the first sparks of lubriciousness.

From an aggressively prudish nurse? Ah, but exactly. The Capelletti knew their daughter, understood her independent — not to say rebellious — nature, and assumed that a prude would be absurd enough to invite rebellion and encourage sexual fantasies in their daughter. This way, they could match her up with anything in pants and assume her eagerness, her whole-hearted enthusiasm. It was a reasonable enough strata- gem which would have worked, I dare say, if Rosaline and I had not interfered. As it was, Giulietta was vulnerable to any advance by any male, wearing pants or not — in my case, let us remember, there was the soutane.

Nurse Caterina was a good woman, pious, simple, wholly deserving of compassion. Her secret, which I wormed out of her in the confessional, was that she had been ravished as a young girl. She hated men, hated sex, but most of all hated the fact that she was ugly, that the rapists had molested her as a joke, and that she could never expect such attentions to be paid her again in a more affectionate context. All the emotion that should have found a humane (not to say human) mode of expression, she directed toward Jesus — which put me into a position of considerable power and authority. She was willing to take any suggestion, follow any instruction, perform any penance — she adored them, actually — I might take it into my head to suggest. For Jesus' sake.

The fact of the matter is that she was far less ugly than she supposed. There are some women — they abound in Italy — who blossom gorgeously in their early teens and then fade to drabness in their twenties and are old women by their mid-thirties. There are others, and Caterina was one of these, who mature slowly, who are insignificant and mousy as teen-aged girls, who begin to acquire character and personality in their twenties and thirties, and who — if their lives have been fortunate and they have been properly nourished and kept free of disease — only come into their own in their forties. They are like some of the better wines, meager and crabby when drunk too young, but generous and rewarding in the fullness of years.

Caterina has only a tangential connection to the story I am telling here, but she is worth dwelling upon for a moment because I remember what I thought about her, how she struck me in those early days, and what I contemplated for her. It is important in this kind of confession to be scrupulously honest. I want neither to exonerate myself nor to wallow in a sentimental excess of guilt. It is a difficult line to walk. But I remember, thinking about Caterina, that it would be a good work, a work of Christian charity, for me to seduce her.

Assume by some fluky turn of events that Rosaline's first project should accomplish itself and that Giulietta should get paired off with the Monteccho lad. Then Caterina would be out of a job. The Capelletti would have no further use for her. The prospects would be less than bright for employment in the Monteccho household. What better for her, then, than a vocation to the Church, a call to one of the more amusing nunneries, a position as a mother superior even?

Seduced, encouraged to the self-confidence to which she was entitled, given a little affection and attention, and put in a position where she could do some good for the world and herself, she might have become someone, might have had some sort of life. It was not an altogether selfish idea on my part. At worst, there may have been a little self-congratulation on my discernment that she was not, after all, so homely as she had been led to think.

I take such pains to make all this clear in order to demonstrate what seems to me just as clear — that I did not have, at this stage, any particular designs upon Giulietta for myself. I entertained the possibility. Or the possibility entertained me. But that happens all the time. What else is the intellect for than to work out possibilities, to construct reasonable sequences by which we may try to estimate the consequences of our actions? In this, the saint and the sinner are united, for though their aims may differ, their need to estimate probable outcomes remains the same. And the limitations on both remain constant — for the event is always surprising, just a little different from what the most prudent man could have predicted — or the wildest man supposed.

For instance, it would not have been my guess at that first meeting that Caterina and I should become friends, perfectly innocent, sympathetic, spontaneous friends. She had to

escort Giulietta to the church twice or thrice weekly for our
discussions, and she would busy herself polishing the silver
— of which the church had an incredible amount, chalices,
pyxes, reliquaries, and God alone knows (or cares) what else.
To this mountain of precious junk she applied herself with
many soft cloths and much polish and perspiration. By the
end of these sessions, she looked quite flushed and handsome,
delicate beads of sweet sweat decking her brow like seed
pearls on a diadem. I would give Giulietta some prayers to
say, and Caterina and I would talk. It was during these talks
of ours that I learned about her childhood molestation, her
parents' disregard for her, the general meanness and meager-
ness of her peasant existence. It was not news, but it is always
news each time it happens to another human being. I listened
attentively, as no man ever had before. And she opened her
heart.

In the meantime, my interest had increased in Giulietta,
because her charm, her liveliness, her intelligence and gaiety
grew upon me like a young vine upon an old wall, making it
green and gaudy. She knew how to beat me at my own game,
answer me right back, silliness for silliness. She had contrived
a wonderful device, for example, for pushing away impure
thoughts. She told me that instead of imagining fornication
with just anyone, she imagined it with me — because I was
a priest and therefore impossible. As far removed from the
world of the flesh as the angels themselves.

"A curious idea," I said, as unsmiling as I could contrive
to remain.

"The only trouble is that I can't imagine what it's like
after the beginning. It's always the same in the beginning.
We're here, in the church, talking, and then one thing leads

to another, and we begin to make love . . . But then it all gets blurry."

"Yes, it does."

"And it's different each time I try to imagine it."

"Yes, it is."

"Oh, Fra Lorenzo, you're teasing me."

"Yes, I am."

"After all, what would you know about it? You're a priest, for God's sake."

"I am, for God's sake. But I hear things. I hear all sorts of things from people with . . . considerable experience."

"I imagine you do," she said, her eyes wide, her lips making a shocked little 0. "Doesn't it bother you?"

"It's the cross I bear."

"And you fight against it."

"I do."

"And you always win," she said. A little pause for effect. "Don't you?"

"Who is instructing whom?" I asked.

"You. Are instructing. Me." With luscious pauses where I have put the stops.

"Pray, pray," I advised her. "You will get stronger. It will get more difficult, but you will get stronger, so it will feel about the same."

"I can't stand it," she said, groaning prettily.

"You must. You must try. Live from one hour to the next, one moment to the next."

"I'll see you on Tuesday."

She went to the apse where Caterina had been polishing and shining, cleaning and brightening, and they took their leave. I waved a blessing at them.

"You pig," I heard. I turned around. It was Rosaline. My

daughter. My only — so far as I know — begotten child. "You incredible pig."

"What on earth are you talking about?"

"You love her." It was an accusation.

I knew immediately that it was true. I remember thinking, and even saying aloud, "How extraordinary."

III

SHE WAS NOT PLEASED. With a singlemindedness I found painful to contemplate in a confederate (never mind that she was a relative), she took the view that any alteration of her original plans was hostile, a nuisance if not a threat. A healthier attitude would have been some willingness to accept innovation as, first of all, inevitable, but also as an opportunity for refinement and improvement. She was uncomfortable in this wonderful condition of dialogue between her wishes and the possibilities and eccentricities of the external world. I remember thinking, early on, that she was not trustworthy — and this was not because I expected her to betray me at any particular point (although that was always a possibility), but because I did not trust her ability, or willingness, to improvise. The real musician is the one who can take a melody and noodle about with it, transpose from one key to another, invert it, change the rhythm, speed it up, slow it down . . . play it! The child who has mastered only the rote performance of what is on the page has learned nothing at all.

But I sermonize. It is an occupational hazard, I fear. Still, it was what I found to think about as she heaped abuse upon me, uttering scatologies, blasphemies, obscenities, and rudenesses that resonated in the vaulting of the church. The effect, while interesting at first, soon diminished. After the first few minutes, I was bored. I waited for her to tire, and eventually she did subside to a level where discourse was possible. I took issue with her about the charge that I was a dirty old man. "It is not dirty to be old. And what you're talking about — lust — is not dirty in the young. It's a stupid term, invented by those who have a dislike of sex and a fear of getting old. It's unworthy of you."

"You must admit, though, a certain disproportion in your ages. You could be her grandfather."

"The perfect age for a lover. Those young men have no finesse. They pride themselves on their energies and animal spirits . . . but it means nothing without finesse. Most of them aren't lovers but fountains."

"Don't be gross."

"You? Tell me? That? After the incredible plainsong I just heard from your very own lips? What cheek! But the fact remains that elder men and younger women are a natural match. Just as younger men and older women accommodate one another with the least possible strain and friction. Indeed, if I were in your place and were being practical and realistic, I'd think of the Montecchio boy for myself. He'd suit you much better than the Prince."

"Don't be absurd."

"Gross. Absurd. You have a way with words, not to mention your beautiful manners. And your respect for your father. I'm telling you the truth about the boy."

"They're merchants."

"You're a snob, eh?"

"At least we're alike in something, then, Father. No?"

It was as close as she was likely to come that day to an expression of affection. I accepted it in that spirit — although I was wrong to do so. She was quite serious in her disapproval of my interest in Giulietta, for the most improbable of reasons: it offended her sense of morality!

Astonishing, but true. One would think that the centuries had whirled backwards, the Renaissance been repealed, and the Middle Ages reestablished, but there it was. Or there she was — a deeply conventional, sincerely conservative young woman. Instead of profiting from the vicissitudes of her early years, learning to bend with the wind and grow like the lilies of the field, she had created an imaginary world in which she attributed to the rich and the powerful a kind of respectability, a simple-minded moral calculus of deserving by which they were in some loony way entitled to all the good things in life because they brushed their teeth, were kind to animals, lit candles in churches, and performed other such good works. It is a dangerous doctrine if pursued to its logical consequences. It is unrealistic and — well, frankly, Protestant. But it was the only way she could account for the manner in which she had begun life as an underprivileged outsider. It had to be her fault.

These were unexamined ideas, and for that matter unexpressed, certainly to me. If I had any notion of the rubbish that was moldering inside her skull, I'd have done something about it. Instead, she appeared, presented herself as my child, and seemed sensible enough (shrewdness and animal cunning will often look like intelligence). I drew unwarranted assumptions about what she was thinking and feeling. Mea culpa.

She listened to little of what I told her, although the part about how she was a reasonable match for the Montecchio boy managed to get through her selective baffles. I suppose we all hear what we are trained to hear. Matchmaking suggestions, no matter how lightly made, she picked up with the acuity of an owl flying at night over a wood where a little vole is scampering. She dove, unerringly and with a terrible greed.

No, that isn't fair. But she did pick up the suggestion,

consider it, try it in various places in the empty spot in the middle of the puzzle, and so find a way she could make it fit with her intention. She would use herself as bait, arouse young Romeo's interest herself, and then pass him on, the way women sometimes do in their mystical consorority, to Giulietta. It was inventive enough, and even had a certain activist charm, but it lacked that adaptability, that flexibility I have been trying to describe. It was too much directed to a certain outcome.

Or perhaps I am objecting — was objecting at the time — because I had begun to sense that her objectives and my own were no longer compatible and might well become mutually exclusive. On the other hand, in my arrogance I assumed that I had more experience than she, was smarter, and could — if a conflict should arise — manage somehow to have my purposes accomplished rather than hers. I assumed what it was reasonable to assume: that my flexibility of purpose was, in itself, an advantage.

She, meanwhile, contrived a meeting with the Monteccho lad.

Romeo, ah Romeo, the famous lover, the beau ideal of Italian manhood. The paragon of selfless passion. Not so, not so. A boor. A lunk. A dunderhead. A lummox who was an embarrassment even to his father, whose standards were minimal at best. The Capelletti, for all their shortcomings, had at least a veneer of civility. The Montecchi were raw wood, not even sanded down; all the rough edges of the upstart and the arriviste offered abrasions if not actual splinters to anyone who had the folly to come too close.

In a way, it was exactly what Rosaline deserved — to have to put up with them, and with Romeo in particular. What she did was send him a note, inviting him to a tryst at the Roman arena (that purlieu of alley-cats, tom-cats, and other assorted felines looking, all of them, gray in the dark). He came not because he thought Rosaline was especially desirable, but because he was convinced that he was such a handsome fellow, such a toothsome morsel, that it was his duty to accommodate women who had the good taste to admire him — or share his high opinion of himself.

His preliminary inspection of Rosaline was cursory but efficient. I did not witness it, of course, but I delight to imagine it. The frank stare in three stages — bosom, hips, face, in whatever order of importance he assigned these areas. She stood there like an animal at auction, like a piece of meat in a butcher's stall, waiting to discover whether she was satisfactory. She was. And immediately he jumped on her and commenced to molest her with the finesse a rooster shows a hen.

"No, no, no, you don't understand," she must have said.

"Oh, I understand," he might well have answered, leering, having it as an established principle that he was too gorgeous to resist, that the only cause for resistance therefore had to be playful, an invitation to force . . . That this barnyard stud has become the paradigm of the exquisite lover, the delicately transported sensibility, the poignant adoration of the young man for his maid, is nothing short of hilarious. It is an epic joke, a metaphysical wonder. And a warning. If Fame is such a buffoon, who wants anything to do with her?

But back to Rosaline, grappling with this garlicky, pomaded, perfumed, under-laundered and over-ardent faun. All the while, as she pried his fingers from her thighs and kept her head in motion to elude his kiss, she was trying to reach the small region of his brain that was not devoted to the procreative act. She claims she was able to reach him before he

had his way with her. I am not sure. I don't believe or disbe-
lieve her. Her testimony is of no weight at all, her motives
being what they were. The only appeal here is to aesthetic
truth — which do I prefer to believe? Which teases me better
or longer or more insidiously? Her single-mindedness was
such that she would have done whatever was necessary to
gain his attention — which was, at best, dim. And knowing
what he was like, I cannot credit him with any willingness to
listen to anything other than praise for his prowess, his size,
his bold mastery, his . . . whatever women of that class learn
to tell their men, even as they make shopping lists or arrange
the seatings for large dinner parties. Afterwards, in the awkward interval even he would have needed for a recovery of
his animal spirits, there would have been an opportunity for
conversation of a more general nature.

It is not mere prurience that motivates these specula-
tions. On the contrary, what people do in the privacy of their
own amphitheaters is their business. But her criticism of my
conduct, morals, and even taste leads me to wonder from
whom this criticism comes. She is not, for all her airs, such a
paragon as she'd like us all to believe. Her reputation in the
folk tales is practically non-existent. She is barely mentioned
and not at all remembered, central though she was to the
development of these peculiar events. It was she, at any rate,
who engineered the meeting. In that post-coital stupor of his,
he allowed himself to be persuaded that there really was a
friend, that Rosaline was not interested in him for herself but
for this friend (she had been carried away by his gorgeous-
ness, the callow fellow thought). The least he could do, then,
was to come and take a look at the girl. If he liked her, fine.
And if not, nothing more would be said. No risk at all on his
side. None. If he was disappointed, didn't like the tilt of her

nose or the curve of her lip, found her for some reason defi-
cient in allure, then Rosaline might make it up to him herself, offering another helping of those sweets he had already
found pleasing. Did she go that far? The fascinating thing is
that I cannot conceive any limits to what she might have done
if she had felt it necessary. That blindered condition of hers
kept her from any sense of proportion, which was another
reason I found it difficult to deal with her.

But whatever she did or said, she managed to convince
him, to capture and hold his attention, and to impress herself upon it deeply enough for him to remember to keep the
appointment they made.

The appointment was for the next day — in my church.
She welcomed him there, secreted him in the confessional
next to the one I habitually used, and relied upon his breed-
ing and manners — or the lack of them — for the rest. Of
course he listened in, eavesdropping on Giulietta's most
intimate revelations of her struggle against concupiscence, her
efforts to avoid thinking about fornication, her nurse's
suggestion that she lie supine with her arms outspread to
form a cross and to avoid the temptation of touching herself
privately, and her confession that, lying there in that position,
she felt as though waiting for some lover, some mysterious
and delightful man to fold her in his arms, to pluck her up,
as she offered herself up to his embrace like a freshly opened
blossom.

She was playing to me, of course. It was a kind of game
we had worked out together, never having to say exactly what
the rules were, but intuiting them, effortlessly exchanging all
the necessary details of what the limits were and how the
thing ought to be conducted. She teased me as I teased her,
and there was a lightness and wit to it Romeo could never

have appreciated, even if someone had tried to explain it to him. Ricotta between the ears, packed tight!

But it got to him, or enough of it did. He just loved to hear her say, "Fornication." He banged his head on the floor in ecstasy (although, alas, not hard enough to split open his cranium).

"Think of Jesus," I counseled her, going pretty far, I admit, in our little game.

"I do," she said. "And I think that he was a most attractive man. A beautiful man."

"The most beautiful man who ever lived," I told her.

"And then I think of the Church," she said. "And then I think of you. And I think of fornication with you."

"Yes, yes. Impossible."

"Yes, impossible!"

And at this, the buffoon, unable to contain himself, betrayed his presence with a groan. Being not only a buffoon but also a coward, he fled — so precipitously that I was unable to see who had been listening.

A Capelletto spy would have stood his ground. Capelletto, himself, would have confronted me. That it could be anyone else didn't even cross my mind. Still, I thought we'd done enough for the day. I summoned her nurse, bade them both God speed, and went to my cell for my private devotions.

Outside, meanwhile, Romeo and Rosaline, in the shadow of one of the buttresses of my own church, were appraising the charms of Giulietta. Romeo needed no persuasion. He was already sold. "But who is it? Who is she? How come I've never seen her before?"

Rosaline explained that the girl was Giulietta Capelletto. He was checked for a moment — but only for a moment. He was not a young man much devoted to principle and honor, so that he would not have been troubled excessively. He paused, thought for a moment, allowed himself — Rosaline told me later — a pensive "Oh, Gee!" And then his brow cleared and he was committed.

The machinery by which to arrange a meeting of the two young people was not complicated. And Romeo had Rosaline's help, anyway, to supply his needs in imaginative thinking.

Certainly, she was devious enough for the two of them. I underestimated her, I've said already (haven't I?). In her position, right then, I'm not sure I'd have thought of doing what she did. She watched Romeo amble down the street, waited for the soiled velvet buttocks to disappear around the corner, and then presented herself to me, pounding upon the door of my cell and disturbing my meditation.

As quickly as I could, I prepared myself to greet her. I was dismayed to hear what she had come to report — that Romeo Monteccho had been hiding in my church, had listened, was struck by the girl and, in fact, was in love with her. "You see?" she said. "It's working. You said it couldn't be managed, but it's all coming together. I have Romeo in love with Giulietta. I've figured out a way of having Giulietta fall in love with Romeo. They will be married. There will be peace in Verona. I will marry the Prince. And you will be named cardinal."

"You're raving."

"No, I'm serious. The Cardinal of Venice died last night. I just heard it from the Prince, who just got the news by special messenger. You'll hear in a day or two, I'm sure."

"Piccolomini? Dead?" I asked.

"Yes. They say it was a surfeit of marzipan. Which could

mean that he was poisoned. Or it could mean that he really died of too much marzipan — but they want us to think it was poison because the other is too embarrassing. Or too funny. Don't you think it's funny?"

"Piccolomini was a friend of mine," I told her. "But that has nothing to do with this. You're absolutely mad, you know."

"No, not at all. I'm saner than anyone in Verona. I'm the only one who has the faintest idea how to bring peace to the city. You just have no imagination."

"I have a perfectly adequate imagination. Preternaturally vivid, in fact," I told her. "But I don't see that the one step follows from the other."

"Which?"

"Any! Besides," I added, "you can't bring people in here to listen to confessions. It's indecent."

"So are the confessions. You ought to be ashamed of yourself. 'Fornication, fornication.'" The last words were in a falsetto that was supposed to mimic Giulietta's voice.

"Shut your mouth!"

"All right, but you'll see. It's working. And I'll make it all happen whether you believe in it or not. You can't have any serious designs on the girl, can you?"

"I don't see why not."

"Because it's . . . frivolous."

"My appetites are frivolous, but yours are serious, is that it? You've got a hell of a nerve," I told her.

"I need it. Even if I were the illegitimate daughter of the Doge, I'd need it. As your illegitimate daughter, it's all I have. Almost all, anyway," she said, patting her hair in a reflexive compliment.

"Is that all, then?" I asked her, impatient to bring the interview to a conclusion.

"Yes, that's all. I just thought I owed it to you to keep you au courant."

If I had paid attention to the grammar instead of that stupid bit of unnecessary French at the end, I might have wondered why she thought she owed me anything. And that, in turn, might have raised the question in my mind as to whether she was doing me a favor or imposing upon me. I might have been only a half step behind her, instead of several leagues.

But I didn't notice. I was eager to return to my solitary contemplations.

Giulietta and her nurse came to visit me two days later, according to schedule. Giulietta and I had another delightful conversation, exploring some of the paradoxes of the celibate life and its opportunity for spiritual exercise and meditation. It is not, as grosser and cruder sensibilities might suppose, a condition of mere frustration, but rather brings its own possibilities for refined exploration of the intertwining of souls, a model for the intercourse of angels in the lower spheres of heaven. We had an altogether delicious hour or so, and afterwards, as was her custom, Giulietta departed in the company of her nurse and protector.

In the street, they were set upon by ruffians. Four thugs, making lewd gestures, appeared out of nowhere and attacked the nurse and the girl. Indeed, they had been waiting for the two of them. In fact, they were Monteccho thugs Romeo had set upon the two females so that he could appear — as he did actually appear, on cue — to fight them off and seem to rescue Giulietta, earning at once her gratitude and admiration.

A nice, quick, clean little stratagem, no? I admit, it had its appeal. It was efficient and simple, and ought to have worked better than it did. What it failed to take into account, because Rosaline didn't know everything — none of us knows everything — was the nurse's history of having been once assaulted, her peculiar combination of fear and rage, and the likelihood, in this particular kind of crisis, of her extreme reaction. She was what one would have called noble — had the attack been real and the thugs been in earnest. As far as she was concerned, Giulietta's honor, Giulietta's life, and her own life were in jeopardy. She fought like a demon, like a fury, like an old Roman heroine.

This had the effect of throwing off the timing of the whole enterprise, because it had been choreographed without expectation of any real resistance or of the thugs being terrified, which wasn't very difficult: they were not the bravest of cavalieri, or even the bravest or most expensive thugs. More likely than not, they were valets and grooms, pressed into service and offered a few scudi for a quarter of an hour's waiting and three minutes' work. But the nurse produced a dagger from the recesses of her skirt and started slashing the air in great semicircles and figure-eights, protecting the girl with her own body. The thugs, surprised by this show of disproportionate force — they knew they were not threatening any real danger — reacted badly. They claimed later that they were trying merely to disarm the nurse before she hurt herself or one of them. This is not impossible. But the result was that one of them stabbed the nurse in the side, a real wound with a real sword, bringing forth real blood.

And real death.

Romeo appeared, brandishing his weapon and forcing the men back and away. They were only too happy to run, to get the hell out of there. Giulietta was, of course, grateful, admiring, all that Rosaline had intended. But the nurse, poor Caterina, was bleeding her life into the gutter.

For her, for the dead nurse, there was nothing to do but mourn. But for Rosaline and for Romeo, there was a different kind of concern. The nurse's death turned them from earnest, ambitious, somewhat blind manipulators into fanatics. They now had the peculiar feeling that any check to their plans was an implied affront to the memory of the nurse — whose life their project had taken. The project now became, in a truly grotesque way, a memorial. This is what sentiment manages to do — and its results are far more cruel than even cynics like me can imagine.

Romeo was, I should think, perturbed. In his aimless, pointless, purposeless life, he had gone from one appetite to the next without a thought of consequence, without any notion of responsibility or limitation, without any feeling that the laws of nature even applied to him. He was amazed by the death of the woman. He was . . . flattered by it. It resonated, and his was the voice in the echo chamber. He took it all as peculiar evidence of his importance. And naturally, he now fell deeply in love with Giulietta — because of the death of the nurse and its flattery.

All the world loves a lover, the saying goes. And Romeo is the world's model lover. But I ask you, who could love that? Who could stand to be in the same tavern, the same street, the same city as that miserable clod tricked out as a lover?

Instant rapture! He adored her. And she, innocent as she was, full of the stuff and garbage of nursery stories and the fanciful projections of the nurse, took his appearance, his rescue, his adoration as fated. That was the way it was supposed to happen. Its authenticity was beyond question because it conformed to her cheap expectations. All her wit, liveliness, and native spirit failed her, because the events conspired to present themselves in exactly the form she'd been told about for years and years.

One could vomit!

But they thought it was just fine. He saw her home, and she invited him inside to meet her parents. He had to decline, and she had to ask why, and finally he had to confess that his name was Romeo Montecchio.

"But I'm a Capelletto."

"I know. But a rose you called something else would smell just as good, wouldn't it? I mean, what difference does it make about names, right?"

Some such piffle. But there would have been a posed look of soul-stricken hang-dog farewell, something out of one of the cheaper painters, and then he would have disappeared.

At this point, Rosaline arrived to let me know what had happened. I was shocked. The bloodshed was bad enough, but worse — far worse — was the way in which I was implicated in it. This was part of a plot that had included me in a peripheral way. I was an accessory, legally if not morally. It would certainly have been most awkward for all the details to come out — about my connection with Rosaline, to begin with. After that, the town would have assumed the worst of all of us, Romeo, Rosaline, and me. I'd have been lucky to keep out of jail. And with my somewhat checkered record, I'd have been transferred to a parish in Sardinia and would have been preaching to bandits and shepherds and living on well water and cheese.

It was impossibly unfair. They had botched it, they had made the mess, but I was the one less free. I criticized her, excoriated her even, but she just sat there and smiled, and then, at the end, asked me whether I thought I could pull out now.

Obviously, I had no choice but to continue. "What do you want me to do?" I inquired, assuming that her further impositions and my involvement would only be getting larger and more perilous.

"Keep the church open tonight. At eleven, we shall begin our vigil."

"A vigil? Is that your next move?" I asked.

"It's out of our hands now. It's Romeo's move. He'll be paying a call upon Giulietta tonight. At eleven. If all goes the way I've arranged it and planned it, they'll be here sometime after that for you to marry them. And then, in the morning, the parents on both sides will have to accept a *fait accompli*."

This time, that fillip of French at the end did not throw me off. I had caught up with her.

IV

RECKLESSNESS IS THE THING. What people adore about the distorted version of the story they have been told so many times is Romeo's recklessness, his beautiful indifference to worldly concerns, even to his own safety, swept away as he was by pure passion.

Pure nonsense! Had Romeo's true position been known, he'd be held up as a model of virtue by cautious fathers to their feckless offspring. Romeo was the model of prudence and circumspection. *What profiteth it a man to gain his beloved's soul if he loseth his own ass?* That could have hung as a sampler over our amoroso's cot. He was not given to epigrams, of course, but the spiritless spirit of the thing would have suited him.

At this point, he needed a confederate. A lookout, first of all. And a spokesperson, as well. He was sufficiently self-aware to recognize his shortcomings in eloquence and courage. He hied himself homeward, therefore, to recruit the aid of his old nanny.

"You want me to . . . what?"

"To go to the Capelletti and offer your services there," he told her.

"Taken one too many knocks on the head, haven't you, dearie?'

"It's part of a plan," he told her, proud of himself for having one.

"I just walk up and offer my services?" she asked.

"That's right," he told her.

"And they'll hire me?"

"That's right," he told her.

"Why? Why would they want to do that?"

"Because they *need* a nurse," he told her, more pleased with himself than ever.

It did not take her all that long to see through his goofy grin. "What happened to the nurse they used to have?"

"She met with a terrible accident."

"She's dead?"

"Yes," he said, still grinning like a baboon.

"Not on your life then," the nurse said, being not quite such a fool as her old charge. "It's dangerous."

"No, no it isn't," he insisted. "I mean, look at it. If you're in the Capelletto household, who do you have to worry about?"

"The Montecchi, I suppose."

"But that's just it. You don't. Because they're us. Or we're them. You know what I'm saying."

"Despite your way of saying it, I think I do."

"Besides," he said, "I'll pay you. I'll pay you . . . whatever you want."

"Whatever I want?"

"Within reason, I mean. I mean, it's going to be good for everybody, see. And, eventually, I'll be able to pay you . . . as much as you want. For the rest of your life, even."

"That's making it sound even more dangerous."

"You don't trust me?"

"Never."

"You won't do it?"

"I didn't say that. But it'll cost you. In advance."

"Oh, boy . . ."

The words I am inventing, but the style of it I am merely reporting. There would have been exactly that kind of low-level bickering, fear and greed warring together in their age-old battlefields of second-rate minds. What matters is that the outcome, inevitable from the beginning, was the nurse's acceptance of his demands and, consequently, her presentation of herself at the Capelletti door to offer her services as nurse.

Bawd, is what she was. Pimp. Pander. Madame. Having spent her tender years in a leaping academy on the banks of the Adige, her ministrations to Romeo were of an indelicate nature, even when the boy was a tiny infant. It was her easy way of soothing him, making him quiet, preventing his yowls from adding insult to the injury of her hangovers. As he grew to young manhood, she found herself more in the role of agent than principal, providing for his lusts from the lists of the servants, the peasants, the dependents, any defenseless female who could be procured through bribery, intimidation, ambition, or even, upon occasion, physical force. He was the placid bull, enclosed in his pen, waiting for the farmer to bring him heifers. No wonder he required her complicity in his wooing of Giulietta. Like a fetishist, he was lost without her presence. Her association with the enterprise was a condition absolutely necessary for his virility to manifest itself.

She was hired, of course. The Capelletti — superstitious in the manner of many of the new rich who distrust the fluke by which they have risen — took her application as a lucky omen. It was meant to be. The coincidence could only mean that God wanted them to hire this woman. Well, somebody did.

Giulietta, stunned by the violence of the day's events and susceptible to the impression Romeo had made, was disoriented by the unaccustomed pressure of having to make decisions.

There was a no-account count to whom she had been unofficially betrothed some years before. Her father, thinking he had made a very good bargain, had bailed out some bankrupt nobleman in a shrewd piece of financial manipulation that did not cost him very much. In exchange, he received a promise of matrimony. His issue would be ennobled. And his ambition would be crowned, or awarded a tiara, by this matrimonial arabesque. She must have been nine at the time of these arrangements. But she knew of them, had lived with them for years. She understood what was expected of her.

On the other hand, here was Romeo. And here was the nurse, insinuated into the bosom of the household like Cleopatra's asp, the venom being her sac of lies and half-truths to lull Giulietta's conscience and allay her fears. The nurse interviewed the young woman. It may have taken thirty seconds to elicit from the girl an account of the murder and the narrow escape of that very day. Probably less than that. It would have been a matter of minutes before the ethical questions arose — about her duty to her father and what she owed Romeo Monteccho, who had saved her life. A second father he was, for if Capelletto had given her life, Romeo had preserved it.

Something like that would have been the wedge the nurse used. And from there, it would have been easy. Capelletto's ambition for noble grandchildren was only a mark of his limited imagination. If Giulietta married Romeo Monteccho, and if there were peace in Verona, he might be made . . . a Knight of Malta. Any number of decorations would be possible, and not for his children and grandchildren, but for himself.

But this is too abstract. There would have been, on the one hand, an intellectual framework for the nurse's suggestions, but the suggestions themselves would have been primarily of a kind that would appeal to a young girl whose mind was full of the clichés of poetry and fiction. Her champion would perhaps come to see her again. Her gallant would, no doubt, risk his honor, his fortune, his life itself, coming to the Capelletto house . . . Soon! Perhaps this very night!

"Oh, my God! What should I do? I'd be so afraid!"

"Afraid? Why? What would you be afraid of?"

"He might attack me? He might . . . rape me?"

"But if you wanted him to, it wouldn't be rape, would it?"

"No! It would be . . . fornication!"

"That's right," the nurse would have said, no doubt startled by the innocent honesty of the girl's locution.

"And that'd be just what I've dreamed about," Giulietta could well have added, even further puzzling the old bawd.

I find it aesthetically and morally fascinating to see how my cultivation of the ground opened Giulietta's mind like a field to the sowing of seeds, any seeds — flower or weed, salubrious grain or deadly nightshade. It did not take intelligence on the nurse's part, or special delicacy or tact. Giulietta did most of the work herself, by herself and to herself. Timing was all — and that was the unpredictable and irrational setting for all our efforts. What balances our superior intelligence and native ability is that indifferent quality of luck, not only blind as the saying goes, but impertinent, disrespectful, obstreperous, and elfin.

In the long run, ability tends to win out. But in the quick

maneuver, there are more variables than the most farsighted and prudent intelligence can possibly account for, and this makes all men, in some sense, equal. It is the secular equivalent of the theological puzzle about how heaven equally fills every unequal cup.

It was, in any event, an amazingly easy thing for the nurse to arouse Giulietta's interest and enlist her cooperation. The window — the famous balcony window — that had formerly been kept locked and bolted, was left open to the fresh air, the scents of flowers, and the winds of fortune. A night light was left burning, even though Giulietta had long outgrown her hobgoblins and witches — for as the nurse assured her, many women, grown-up, adult women, use night lights.

"But whatever for?" I can hear the slip of a thing inquire.

"For finding things. Or for being found," I can just as readily hear the whoremonger reply.

"Being found?"

"How would you feel if Romeo were to come looking for you, were to fall over a chair, were to break his leg . . . ?

"Oh, that'd be awful!"

"Absolutely. That's why women have night lights."

"But that's wicked."

"No, on the contrary. It's kind."

"I can see that, yes. Yes, that would follow, wouldn't it. It's wicked, but it's kind."

Thus innocence is put upon. There may have been other objections the young girl raised, but each would have been answered, confused, confounded, or refuted by the old flesh-peddler. There could have been moments of backsliding, but there she'd be with her assurances, encouragements, and endorsements. And that woman was, let us remember, in a position of authority. The girl's welfare had been put into her hands. She had inherited the august mantle of her lamented predecessor. It was easier than taking candy from a baby. It was giving candy to a baby.

And that night, he showed up with a rope coiled about his middle. He must have looked like an errant alpinist. Or a burglar. Or perhaps a suicide, in search of an appropriately situated and sufficiently lofty tree. The rope was unnecessary. The balcony was nowhere near so high as Romeo — and the folklore — supposed. Indeed, it was a rather low, quite accessible balcony, having been designed by the previous owner to accommodate his own late entry into his house, without awkward noises from the dogs or questions from his wife. It was architecturally uninteresting, so much so that — I am told — tourists have rebelled and the guides have agreed to point out another, likelier looking balcony on another building as *the* balcony on which Giulietta stood and up to which Romeo gazed and, at length, climbed. But not even at that balcony, with its little balustrade and its graceful, rather Moorish arch, would Romeo have needed that rope. A muleteer looking for his strayed animals, or an apprentice fakir looking for a master who might teach him to make the rope stand up and climb it, thus our Romeo made his clown-ish appearance. The rope is never mentioned. But it was there, a cause of some puzzlement and not a little laughter, later on.

Ah, well. We don't have to do the scene, do we? He throws gravel. She opens the window. He looks up and grunts, or caterwauls, or simply looks mutely and imploringly, like a puppy of some large, ungainly breed, hoping for a tidbit. And she, looking down, sees next to nothing, transforms the unimpressive bumbler into the figure she has imagined and been taught to expect, smoothing him out and prettying him up until what she sees is very like the representation on stages. It is a triumph of imagination over reality, of education over perception, of sensibility over sense.

What they actually said cannot possibly matter and would be too painfully banal to recount. The sighs and moans of the lust-struck are invariably amusing to those who are, at that particular instant, sane. What counts is that he had come at the appointed time — having set this up beforehand with his nurse, who was acting as lookout. It was also known, you will recall, to Rosaline, that Pierian spring of his thought and scheme. And she, being, after all, human, with the frailties and imperfections attendant upon that condition, had blabbed to me. She had told me just a bit more than she needed to, and the difference was crucial.

I knew they had coordinated the hour of his wooing, but Romeo didn't know I knew. I betook myself to the belltower of the church and waited there imagining his progress. I allowed him rope, and then, when the time came, grabbed some ropes of my own, which I commenced to tug — sounding an alarum that was ambiguous in its import (fire? attack? a victory in some war about which, through some inadvertence, we had never been informed?) but clear in its urgency. At once, dark windows showed lights. Men and women scurried into the streets like ants from a disturbed hill, dogs barked, sentries challenged, babies cried . . . And Romeo struggled to get away, to break from Giulietta's embrace, to avoid the prickers on the roses that were espaliered on the wall beside the balcony, to elude the Capelletti watchdogs that were barking, answering the barking of all the other dogs in Verona.

I yanked the bellropes like a man possessed. I was possessed, quite rapturously, by the image of Romeo running for his life. The boy was not brave, and neither was he cunning. He needed to get to the street, and perhaps to the corner, but once there, he was quite safe. He could have lost himself in the crowd. He could have run as if after someone. He could have stopped to see why other people were running. He did none of these things. Instead, he assumed — stupidly but correctly — that he was the cause of this uproar, that it was designed, that its object was his discomfiture. And he ran like a rabbit, seeking safety, protection, a place to hide. Sanctuary.

The church. That is, my church.

As I assumed, all along, he would.

I didn't depend upon it and could have improvised had he gone elsewhere, but it was an added convenience, a sort of refinement of which I was proud. And I was enormously pleased when he showed up, bellowing "Sanctuary!" as he thought he was supposed to do. It was stupid — and I enjoyed it, both his obtuseness and my acuity. They were complementary, more or less.

He was at first breathless, then incoherent, then paranoid. He was convinced he'd been betrayed. There were enemies everywhere!

One day, I must devote myself to that peculiar conviction — not at all original with Romeo — that the rest of the world cares enough to bother to conspire against one. If the sin of pride ever makes itself manifest in the lives of ordinary human beings — not princes and popes, but the people one passes in the streets — it is surely in this kind of belief. The certainty that the energies of the rest of mankind are devoted to the persecution of oneself may not, in fact, be pleasant, but it is sinful, nevertheless. Indeed, I wonder whence comes the

notion that all sins are delicious, comfortable, desirable —
they are only prohibited.

But another day. There will be many days. It will be
something to occupy me for a while.

There Romeo was, arrogantly supposing that the rest of
Verona was in hot pursuit, and bellowing for sanctuary.

"Sanctuary, sanctuary!"

"At whom are you yelling?" I asked him.

"Sanctuary!"

"Stop that, or I'll throw you out on the streets where
you belong."

"Please?"

"You're here, aren't you? They can't arrest you inside a
church. You already have sanctuary. Just stop that awful
bellowing. And get up."

He was groveling on the floor, prone, in what he supposed was the position of suppliants. (The true suppliant does
not pay attention to — and cannot afford to worry about —
what position to assume.)

"There were bells," he said, like a puzzled and somewhat
petulant child.

"Yes, I know."

"Everybody was running after me."

"No, they were running at the same time as you. And
in all directions."

"You think?"

"I know. I rang the bells"

"You?" It was not so much a question as a roar of pain
and shock. He drew it out to a kind of moan.

"But why?"

I was about to explain, but at this point we were interrupted by a banging upon the door. He looked about,

convinced that he had been betrayed again, searching for an avenue of escape or a place of concealment.

"The confessional?" I suggested.

He scuttled away to hide. The knocking at the door was repeated. I held off until Romeo was concealed and then called, "Coming, coming!"

"You bastard!" Rosaline spat.

"I'm afraid you have the advantage of me," I said, smiling. "But come in, come in."

"Where is Romeo?"

"Here," I told her. And I called out to the cowering coxcomb, "It's safe. You can come out now."

He didn't trust me. He peeped out shyly, then emerged, looking around as if Rosaline might have brought some of his pursuers with her into the church.

"What is going on? What happened?" Rosaline asked.

"As I was about to explain to your genial oaf, here. . ."

"Wait a minute!" he protested.

"Silence," I commanded. "I did this for your own good. For both of you. For all of you, including Giulietta."

"They could have been married by now," Rosaline said.

"And?" I asked. "You think that would have been sufficient? You think that would have accomplished what you set out to achieve? If you do, you are a bigger fool than I could have supposed."

"If you had objections, you should have let me know them before this," she said, hot with self-righteousness.

"I believe I did. And it was of no use whatever. You went right ahead, involving me as an accessory to this idiot's useless murder."

Romeo opened his mouth to object, but he showed

enough good sense to close it again, leaving the impression of some large fish gaping in its tank.

"I was joined in these absurd proceedings without my consent or approval," I continued. "But having been recruited as a partner, I take it upon myself to exercise all the rights and privileges of a partner — including independent action when it becomes necessary."

"What independent action? Betraying us? Ringing your damned bell?"

"Don't blaspheme in church."

"Oh, for God's sake!"

"Exactly," I said, with infuriating composure.

"I'm sorry," she said, taking a deep breath. "But you can understand how upset I am. It came as something of a shock to discover that my own father was a maniac and would decide to practice bell-ringing. . ."

"Your father?" Romeo asked.

"That was indiscrete," I suggested to my daughter.

"You two are in this together. I don't know what your game is, but . . . but I'll get you. I'll get you both."

As it was his habit to see combinations and conspiracies everywhere, this revelation could not have been reassuring to him. It was, in the long run, unhealthy. But that comes later.

"If you will permit me," I said, shutting him up not so much with my words as with my presence — men of a certain avoirdupois have a presence that can be employed like a cudgel. "The trouble with the plan in its original and, if I may be blunt, primitive version, was that it lacked effect. It did not startle or astonish. It was not commanding enough to jar people from the ruts of their ordinary behavior."

"But it was better than what we have now," Rosaline said. "This is just a shambles."

"He doesn't add much to a salon, does he?" I was being mischievous, twitting Romeo, only because he took it so badly. "Still, we are in no great disarray. It can be made to seem perfectly reasonable. Go now to the Prince . . ."

"The Prince?" Romeo asked. "What has the Prince got to do with this?"

"Oh, shut up," Rosaline said.

"It's all quite simple," I said. "Just so long as you both do as I say, all will be well. Everything will come out right in the end. You see, I've figured out a way of actually bringing it off . . . "

"I don't trust you," Rosaline said.

"Neither do I," Romeo said.

"All right," I said. "Don't. Just quit. Leave. Go and leave me alone. Pretend that nothing ever happened. That will be just fine with me."

"But they're out there, looking for me," Romeo said, not quite whining.

"We can't stop," Rosaline insisted.

"Precisely. And if you can't stop, you must go on. That's logical, isn't it?"

"And what do you want me to tell the Prince?" she asked, admitting that I had won the round."

"Tell him," I said, speaking slowly and deliberately, drawing it out and having fun, "that you have arranged the marriage of Romeo and Giulietta."

"But that's absurd," she said.

"Yes, it is. But the Prince will be pleased with you. And displeased with Capelletto for interfering."

"So? Where will that get us."

"You'll see when we get there," I told her. "You, meanwhile," I told Romeo, "go home and pack."

"Me? Leave here? Go out there?"

"You go. Me stay." Sometimes one has to descend to an abysmal level in order to be understood. "Here, take this," I said, and I offered him a monk's habit with a very large hood. "You'll be safe enough in this."

"I still don't trust you."

"We've already gone through that, haven't we? You'll be all right at home. And by the time Rosaline and I have got things arranged, it will be safe for you to reappear."

He hesitated. I opened the door. He put on the hooded habit. Rosaline and I nudged him out into the street.

Once he was gone, Rosaline wanted a fuller explanation, but I was disinclined to enlighten her immediately. I wanted her to believe me, and it was better, therefore, if I let her coax it from me, one juicy detail after another. In fact, what she threatened to do was go to the Prince and confess all. She would tell him everything — even her complicity in the plot, the point of which was, after all, to bring harmony to the city — and throw herself upon his mercy and his love.

"And you'd be exactly where you were when you started."

"At least I'd be no worse off."

"Nothing ventured, nothing gained," I told her. (Where is that from? The Bible?)

Still, it was a plausible threat she had made. And I could plausibly cave in before it. "This notion about the amity that must flow between the Capelletti and the Montecchi because they are in-laws is madness. People who begin as friends can be turned into enemies through matrimony. Families that have never seen one another are often joined together in intimate hatred that lasts for generations after the recitation of the vows. And you are relying upon this rite to provide even a brief similacrum of friendship? You're wrong. Love won't do it. Marriage won't do it. Not even grandchildren will do what you want. You need something reliable, something foolproof. And in the Church, we have learned that the only reliable maneuver for something like this is martyrdom."

"What?" she may well have actually said. But one needs something like this to break the long dreary paragraph of argument, doesn't one.

"Alive," I continued, "Romeo and Giulietta are just a couple of snotty kids. Dead, they are martyrs. To love. To Veronese quarreling. To any damned thing you want. That will bring peace. Or a little peace, anyway."

"You're going to kill them?" she asked. She really did ask that.

"If it were necessary, I would," I said. "But it isn't. We'll improvise."

V

PICCOLOMINI WAS DEAD. Remember him? Nicolo Piccolomini, friend of my boyhood and Cardinal of Venice, had passed away. And this news that Rosaline had brought and that the couriers of the Church had confirmed complicated my position. One must know what one wants. And given two contradictory goals, one must decide how to proceed, delaying until the last possible moment the choice that nips one bud in order to let the other thrive. Realistically, my chances for the biretta were not good. The corruption of the Church, the claims of Nepos and Simon upon the attentions of the Pontiff, the conservative tendencies of the Curia that looked to services rendered rather than sheer promise and ability, the simple distance of Verona from Rome. These and other disadvantages combined against me.

Still, there was the frisson of irrepressible hope that somehow, against all odds, some prince of the Church might have noticed me, that some intricate process of discussion among the Holy Father's advisors might stall, that some irreconcilable difference might leave them with no hope of a solution in the choice between two well-connected candidates, so that a third, a compromise, might be named — an unlikely but deserving fellow whom several had approvingly noticed but no one had actually talked about. In some such way, in my vivid daydreams, I could see them, hear them, positively feel them coming to a happy agreement about — me. Why not? What is it, after all, that messengers of the Lord always hear from those who have been chosen? "Oh Lord, I am not worthy!" You can look it up! It's almost a conventional remark. And with me, it would be true. I wasn't worthy, knew I wasn't worthy, but saw in my unworthiness as likely a credential as any other.

There wasn't anything I could do about it in an active way. But there was a calming effect, a kind of caution I felt, a degree of restraint and concern I might not otherwise have experienced. The daydream was there, buzzing in a faubourg of my brain, teasing me . . .

And then the news came, to me before it came to the Prince, that a successor had been named, a new cardinal, a new prince of the Church — an eight-year-old boy! A *coup de théâtre*. A *coup de foudre*! Eight! Which of us could hope to outlive an eight-year-old? Which was, of course, the very point of the appointment. That must have been what they were thinking about in the Curia — if they were thinking about anything at all. Perhaps it was just a lottery, a thousand names written on slips of paper, and the Pope picking one of them from a large barrel.

No, that's unlikely. Eight years old though he may have been, he was nevertheless a Schiavone, related to several members of the Council of Ten, to the Doge and, on his mother's side, to the Pope. But that was the reason for the selection of that eight-year-old rather than any other eight-year-old. This was, however, secondary to the purpose of intimidating the rest of us, chastising our ambitions, reproving us for our daydreams. (I was not, I suspect, the only daydreamer.)

Disappointed, I was also liberated. Let Giovanni Schiavone have the biretta. My purposes clarified, my cautions being now beside the point, my inhibitions dissolved, I could actively seek my own reward.

The girl was what I wanted. More and more clearly, I had come to understand that and to recognize in myself uncharacteristic feelings of jealousy in regard to Romeo's importunate suit, Giulietta's receptivity, and the somewhat theoretical prospect of their union. I hated the idea. And I loved her. And at my age, to feel such tenderness, such excitement, such lively longing was a cause for exultation. It was like the blossoming of the crocus in early spring, as surprising as it is beautiful, beautiful because it is so surprising. The years and their cynicism fell away from me like dust on the sill of a window someone's whim has opened.

A wonderful time in a man's life, having that feeling return so poignantly, but I could have resisted it — I might have been willing to fight against it — had it not been for Rosaline's machinations involving me far beyond the limits of prudence. What was the point of my exercising restraint and circumspection on my own, when my ambitious daughter could at any moment bring the whole edifice down about all our ears? The only reasonable thing to do, it seemed, was to salvage what I could, snatch what pleasure I could — however ephemeral — from the slavering jaws of time and circumstance. The nomination of young Schiavone was the last straw. I decided to risk all — because all was already at risk.

The instrumentality of my plan was — as most of the world by now knows — a mysterious potion that induces so deep a sleep as to approximate the great sleep, the permanent one of death. I had the recipe for this decoction from an old abbot who got it from a Spanish friar who actually

knew the great Ambrosio, who invented it. Ambrosio's
ambrosia! Really great stuff.

The story is that Ambrosio was in love with a woman
who was — unbeknownst to him — his twin sister. I've often
wondered whether that makes it better or worse. He was an
abbot, and for him to have been in love with any woman was
sinful. So it might just as well have been incestuous. And that
she was a twin sister, a female self . . . gives it, I think, a curious fascination. Which of us has not wondered what life
would have been like in the other gender? Who wouldn't
jump at the chance of meeting that radically changed but still
recognizable self? Not only could one learn about that other
experience, which just eluded one, but there would be the
more intimate and shameful question — only the bravest
would have the heart to ask — whether one would find oneself attractive. The great rack upon which we are all torn is
the profound otherness of women, is it not? They are us, our
mothers and wives and sisters, but they are non-us, thinking
differently, seeing the world differently, living, as it were, in
another world, where their forms of thought and feeling are
the norm and ours are foreign and not quite knowable. There
is a yawning chasm between us, a great gulf.

Ambrosio, I must suppose, recognizing in his twin sister
some instant affinity, some immediate sympathy, a cordial and
generous intuitiveness that bridged that abyss of difference,
leapt at the chance, responded with preternatural alacrity and
ardor. He felt a kind of homecoming that we wanderers
dream of, all of us, from Adam's fall. His sister was forbidden, but she was a part of him, as much an extension of his
own self as Mother Eve was of Adam.

They snigger when they tell his story. They sniggered
when they told it to me. But they were wrong. After long

contemplation and careful reflection, I am convinced that there was something noble and instructive in Ambrosio's passion. That it was an impossible passion is only a part of the tragedy of mankind, a sign of our fallen state, an indication of the limitation under which we struggle. But our inability to achieve perfection does not mean that some of us, from time to time, do not get glimpses of it, inklings, and in chance encounters see its fugitive possibility. I am sure Ambrosio, chasing after his chaste sister, was chasing after nothing less than this.

She was a devout and chaste woman whose purity and goodness did not indict Ambrosio so much as throw a charitable light upon his depravity. For years, from the time he was a theological student in Madrid, he had known the pleasures of the flesh, submitting to his superiors, the fathers and the monsignors and the abbots, as everyone did. He learned the way to climb over the walls and through the tunnels, out of the seminary and the cloister and into the gay life of the town, the bordellos and taverns and bazaars . . . It is an old story, hardly worth the telling. But Ambrosio was a bright young man, shrewd enough to know his value, attractive enough to allow his shrewdness some room for maneuver. He became a priest, and ascended the ladder of influence and power as all poor boys who join the Church hope to do. But it costs. A little piece of your soul gets torn up, like a ticket, at each gateway. By the time one has risen high enough to do some good, the good that was in one is long gone, its fitful spasms only its death throes.

Imagine, then, the shock, the spiritual refreshment in finding this creature like to an angel that was, in some way, his familiar. He had no idea why this was so, did not learn until later that she was his twin. But his Angela was as necessary to him as the food he ate, the water he drank, or the air he breathed. He followed her, courted her, importuned like the very model of a Petrarchan fool — and each rebuff only fanned the fires of his torment hotter, showing him yet once more how pure and good and desirable she was. He had to have her!

There were, at this time, still Moors in Spain. Infidels, you say, but they were a people of great cleverness. Their mathematics and their medicine were inestimable — although we now think of much of their cunning as witchcraft and black magic. I am not so sure. Ambrosio, driven as he was by a desperation I hope never to know myself, had no scruples, could not afford the luxury of conscience, but betook himself to Seville, where he sought out one of the Moorish pharmacists to aid him in his quest. There had to be a potion, an elixir, some essence or tincture or compound that would charm the senses, lull the conscience, weaken the will . . .

God knows — or the Devil, more likely — what Ambrosio may have had in mind. There was nothing under heaven able to do what he wanted the medicine to do. But there was something, a draught that could approximate death. It was dangerous. It slowed down the functions of the body, the breathing and the beating of the heart, to an indetectable minimum, but in order to do this there was a shock to the system and a risk that an overdose might absolutely interfere with vital functions. Still, it was a way of getting her to the crypt of the nunnery that adjoined Ambrosio's monastery. He could have her there alone in his power, and he figured that he could force her to his will, and then train her to it, teach her to love him, patiently indoctrinating as well as inseminating her.

A loathsome plan? Assuredly. A foul, unspeakable, and contemptible stratagem! As Ambrosio perfectly well knew. He understood how he would be offending not only Angela but the angels who protected her, the heavens she exemplified on earth. It was a scandalous, an utterly heinous plan — but with irresistible force it struck him that it would be a challenge to her goodness, that his badness could hope for forgiveness from her virtue, and that if he could not obtain charity from her, he was doomed to the eternal fires of hell because the Day of Judgment would not look with any greater kindliness upon him than she had. And if he was damned, if it truly was his fate to be cast into the torments of Satan's pits, then — out of pride — he wanted his sin to be sufficiently black as to prevent him from any thought of appeal from that judgment.

But no man believes himself to be utterly beyond hope of salvation. I cannot think but that Ambrosio had a notion, however tenuous and vague, that she would find a way to forgive him, that she would recognize in him that other self and cleave to it. He knew he would be risking her life — but if her life was his happiness, his hope of heaven itself, did he not have the right to risk what was his? We are trained in these casuistries, learn them in boyhood, are taught to dispute with the skill and grace of Aquinas himself. But when the mind is loosed from its tether, that skill becomes terrible. It is like fire, man's friend, gone wild, consuming households, villages, towns . . .

He persuaded himself that it could work, that its hateful qualities would be forgiven, its dangers survived. For Angela, he would risk anything — even Angela. He bought the potion and returned to Madrid. I say the potion, meaning the recipe for the potion. The ingredients took more time and money and effort to assemble. It took him months to get his hands on the herbs and the minerals and the queer equipment necessary for the concoction of this perilous draught. And all the time, he must have wrestled terribly with his conscience, his guilt, his despair, his hope of salvation, his love of Angela, his feelings of solitude in the world, his terrible sense of having been cut off, of being unlike all other men in the history of the universe . . . and worse than any of them.

What he did was to administer the potion exactly as he had been instructed. And then he had another difficult time, no longer struggling actively but now waiting, absolutely helpless, passive, unable to do anything but hope — prayer had been beyond him for some time — that he hadn't really killed her, that she would survive. And even then, he must have wavered, must have wondered whether her death might not be better after all. That way, she would avoid the fate worse than death that he had in store for her. He, of course, would go to hell — as he deserved to do. But she would be saved, would be spared the humiliation and the pain of confronting his depravity. And he would be in part saved by her salvation. Trickier and trickier, and at the same time more and more despairing, he sat through the night in a vigil of a most terrible kind — until the prescribed time had elapsed. And then, with his key, he made his way through the secret passage and into the crypt of the Convent of the Sacred Heart, where he and the mother superior had once disported themselves.

And Angela had lived. He saw her revive. And he persuaded himself upon her, as the Platonic forms persuade themselves upon the flux. And they lived happily ever after. Or they both perished in disgrace and torment, and were consigned to hell. It depends on which version of the story one believes. I've heard it told both ways. The trouble is that it is an example, a demonstration of whatever doctrine or philosophy the teller holds.

The only element that all the versions share in common after that defloration in the convent crypt is their discovery — later on, in the raptures of their bliss or the leisure of their torments — of their relationship as twins, confirming the special intimacy of their love, and — to a degree — explaining the passion that would stop at nothing.

What would one not do to preserve his eyes, his hands, his feet? And yet in none of these does the self repose. Blinded or maimed, a self remains. But for Ambrosio, she was his self, a part of that self so great that the remainder — what was entirely his own — would die without it. It is either a cautionary tale or an ideal example, depending upon your tastes in politics and religion. And in love, too.

*   *   *

I have always loved that story. In my occasional periods of celibacy, it has been a consolation and a comfort to me. On the other hand, during those times in my life when I have been taken with a woman, it was almost as much a consolation to know that other people had been afflicted worse than I. In any event, and for all seasons, there it was with its emotional succor and its practical uses too — for along with the narrative, I had learned the recipe. Ambrosio passed it on before his death, sharing his secret with his brothers in Christ, who reciprocated by strangling him before lighting the faggots, a kindness that is not always extended by the Inquisition.

Acting responsibly, though, I had to allow for the possibility that the proportions had been garbled as the recipe was passed down from father to father over the years. Or that the ingredients had been incompletely enumerated by Ambrosio in the heat of the moment. I had to experiment with it, demonstrating that it could work. As a young man, I tried it with pigs, adjusting the amount of the potion to the weight of the pig. Too little, and the pig merely slept; too much, and the pig died; but just a little less than too much was very impressive in its effect. Having satisfied myself that it was dangerous but possible, I then put the potion to use when I staged the assassination of a very dear friend in Cremona, impressing my superiors, delighting the duke, and displaying my ardent loyalty to Church and state while doing no permanent harm to my friend, who came through it just fine, recovering and immediately departing for Rimini.

The point is that I hadn't used the potion lightly or irresponsibly. That one time in Cremona was special in that if I hadn't offered him the potion, one of the duke's men or one of the bishop's would have given him real poison or real steel. And I would have been not only distressed but embarrassed by a series of irresponsible and all but groundless charges.

But this is hardly the place to go into all that.

What I had to face was the possibility of Giulietta's marrying that galoot, that oaf, that ape. That seemed to me a disaster of such scale as to justify my interference and the risk of the desperate measures I had in mind to employ. Besides, the plan I had worked out was so clever, so irresistibly symmetrical, and of such aesthetic appeal, that I was entranced. Only a philistine could have failed to respond to it. Having conceived it, I could not possibly commit the vandalism of allowing it to be stillborn. That was the whole idea of the Renaissance, wasn't it? Art and all that?

Well, it isn't just paints and canvases and marble and chisels. Leonardo himself has demonstrated — to the point of silliness — that anything can be art. How else do you explain the way he has occupied himself in the Vatican with the construction of toy birds that actually fly around the room? Finally, one wants to construct a thing that will do something, that will move.

I delighted in the idea of people moving around Verona to my will rather than their own, of their speaking words they did not fully understand, which produced effects only I could foresee. For a man of the cloth, I had the peculiarly enlightening and delightful opportunity of glimpsing what human endeavor must seem to the angels in heaven who understand what we cannot understand, who see around corners and through the walls that limit us so severely. It was difficult to restrain a high, shrill, utterly joyous shriek of pleasure as I closed my eyes and saw it all, saw more than they could see, in their rooms and gardens and offices, those flimsy stage sets for my script.

Romeo Montecchio was telling his father that after years of indolence, uselessness, and distraction, he had at last found himself, had set a course for himself, and was about to accomplish great things. Old Montecchio found this difficult to credit, having seen his son come darting through the gates, looking furtively behind him, and only from the interior safety of the courtyard risking the revelation of his identity by the removal of the capacious hood of the habit I'd given him. It didn't exactly look as though he'd set forth on a program of lofty accomplishment and noble resolve.

"Oh?"

"Yes! I know it's something of a surprise, but I've seen the light."

"In that hood?"

"No, no. Inside. In here," he said, pointing to his temple. His father stared at him. In the past, Romeo had been slower than some, but sane. Now? The father was not so sure. "What in the hell are you talking about?"

"I'm going to get married."

"What? To whom?"

"Giulietta Capelletto."

"Good God! Why?"

"Wouldn't it be great?"

"No. I don't know. Does Capelletto know?"

"No, not yet. I don't know. I don't think so. Maybe."

"What do I do? Pick one of those answers?"

"I don't know."

"What's the point of your marrying her?"

"Well, for one thing, I love her," Romeo explained.

"And?"

"And . . . it'd bring peace to Verona."

"No it wouldn't."

"It wouldn't?"

"No."

"Oh. Even so."

"Even so, what?" the father asked.

"I still love her. And it's what I'm going to do."

"Of course, it would screw up Capelletto's plans for Giulietta's marriage."

"He's got plans?" the boy asked.

"I'm sure he has plans. I don't know what they are, but it doesn't matter. If you married her, it'd be . . . it'd be like pissing into his well."

"You mean, you approve?"

"I'm not sure. Why can't you just piss into his well and let it go at that?"

And so on. I had not instructed Romeo to tell his father what he was about to attempt. I felt quite serene, as when I contemplate a move at chess, knowing that he would do this without my having to say anything, that my willing of it was sufficient. Even if he were inclined to resist, his father would interrogate him, examine him, prod and poke until the truth — or all that Romeo knew of it — was out. Simply from a consideration of Romeo's situation and his character, I could predict what he would do. And then, as in chess, I could see where that would inevitably lead, looking ahead to the next move, which would be Montecchio's.

Not sure whether he was winning the upper hand over Capelletto or losing it, whether he was outwitting or out-witted, he would have to stew in the sour sweat of petty scheming until he saw that the obvious maneuver was to go, himself, to Capelletto, try to discover what Capelletto wanted, and then set his own course in an opposite direction. There was a Copernican simplicity to all of this. Each of them thought himself to be an independent Ptolemaic sphere, freely swinging on an autonomous path. But I was the Copernican sun, and they all whirled in their predestined paths around me, around me, around me . . .

The conjunction of Montecchio and Capelletto was delightfully inevitable — and I had spoken not a word, not a syllable or phoneme to either of them. Nevertheless, like marionettes they extended to one another the hollow ritual courtesies, the uninterested inquiries as to health and family, the insincere compliments upon each other's prosperity. And then they began to get down to business. Montecchio would have had to be blunt about it, there being no way of asking, by the bye, whether Capelletto knew about the intention of their children to marry. He'd have just popped it.

"What?!"

"It's what Romeo tells me."

"He's crazy."

"I don't think so."

"I haven't heard anything about it from Giulietta. And she'd tell me. She wouldn't . . . She couldn't . . . She's engaged. To the Parigi boy from Lucca."

"It seems that she may have had second thoughts," Monteccho twitted.

"Never. She would not disobey her father. She would not disappoint her fiancé. And she would not throw herself away."

Which would have begun the escalating series of insults and counter-insults, an old ritual the two of them had refined, by frequent practice, to an impressive level. But it is not absolutely relevant to my purpose here to transcribe the piquant example of ethnography their exchange provided.

More to the point was the other conversation, going on at the same time in another part of the city — in the Scaligeri palace, to be exact, where the Prince was listening to Rosaline's recitation. This, of course, I had prompted, instructing her carefully in what to say.

The Prince, I have to point out, is a rather amiable, very bland fellow who manages to be all but invisible even in his showy ceremonial dress. Or, on second thought, he is especially invisible in his ceremonial dress because all one sees is the uniform with the sashes, the decorations, the ribbons, and the epaulettes with the plaited gold braid festooned back and forth. He could just as easily hire someone of his size and build to stand there in that finery — no one would notice that the occupant was different.

The Prince, moreover, was a Veronese patriot — which is ridiculous on its face. There were the Venetians, who ran the Veneto, and Verona with it. There were Milanese agents, Florentine agents, Bolognese agents, and agents of the Vatican, each looking out for his own interests and working against the interests of all the others. The Prince, having been born to his high office, having experienced no checks in his growth and development, having found no necessity for deviousness or intrigue, disapproved of all these departures from the staunch sincerity he hoped to exemplify — and he generally behaved like a moron, taking people at their word, expecting people to take him at his word, and acting in a manner I can only call un-Italian.

When Rosaline informed him that she had engineered a match between Romeo and Giulietta, he did not doubt her. He was surprised perhaps, but he was pleased. He shared my own doubts about the prospects of this marriage for a peaceful Verona. But he understood Rosaline's motives. He knew she wanted to engineer a state of equilibrium in order to earn his gratitude and, at the same time, free him to marry her.

Amusingly, Rosaline misinterpreted what the Prince meant because he always said exactly what he meant, neither more nor less. He made no promises of marriage, had never made any promise of any kind. But she assumed, because he seemed pleased, that he was comfortable with what she considered to be an unspoken bargain.

The Prince did what he thought right, ceremonially speaking — which is the first consideration among princes. He sent flowers. To Giulietta. And a card with his crest on it and his good wishes to her and to her parents.

This in effect put Capelletto on notice that Monteccho's was not an idle or empty threat. It was, at the very least, part of some general campaign, the point of which had to be what the point always was — the embarrassment of the Capelletti and the abuse of himself.

Capelletto's reaction to this — also predicted by myself — was to lock up Giulietta and her nurse, put a guard at the door, and post more guards out in the streets and in the courtyard. Romeo's paranoia was now an accurate and objective appraisal of the facts as they stood: any of the Capelletti would have set upon him, would have tried to kill him. Fortunately, he returned to my church without mishap, wearing the habit and the hood.

Rosaline returned from her interview with the Prince. It was gratifying indeed for me to be able to tell them what had happened to each of them since they had last been in my company. It was also quite charming to see their look of mystification and puzzlement.

"But what have we accomplished? Giulietta, as you say, is now under guard, locked up, virtually a prisoner," Rosaline complained.

"Indeed," I said. "As she must be."

"But how is she to get out?"

"She isn't. I will go to her. You forget that I am her spiritual advisor. I will go to her to offer her comfort, and to let her know the importance of the sixth commandment, which tells us that we must honor our father and our mother."

"Oh?" Rosaline asked. "And then?"

"I will give her this," I said, holding aloft a phial full of a liquid of a most ominous green color and a repellent, even feculent smell.

"What's that?" Romeo wanted to know.

I explained the properties of the preparation, hurrying perhaps over some of the risks and side-effects, and stressing the benefits to all of us — but is that not the common practice of pharmacologists?

"She will appear to be dead," I said in my dramatic peroration. "Capelletto will be stricken with grief and remorse. Furthermore, he will bring the body here for the requiem mass. And it will be here, in this church, that she will recover. You will be with her. Off you will go, the two of you, to Mantua or Padua or wherever you like. And peace will, indeed, be established in Verona."

"You're sure it works?" Romeo wanted to know.

"Of course," I reassured him.

"It's very . . . green."

"Yes, that's correct. Green is the color. But it is the function rather than the appearance to which I direct your attention. And the result — which will be the fair maiden for you, the hand of the Prince for you, and the thanks of both the churchly and the secular authorities for me."

"It could work, couldn't it?" Rosaline said, won over at last.

"Of course," I said. But I had my fingers crossed.

ROMEO'S FEAR WAS SUCH that he wasn't about to leave the safety — the sanctuary — of the church. So he wasn't going to tell anybody anything. And I could also rely upon Rosaline to keep our confidence, as long as she was convinced that her interests and mine were consonant. Ideally, I shouldn't have told anybody anything. But the ideal is so very difficult. The trouble with Mr. Machiavelli's system, you see, is that it excludes all but the cleverest and the most adept, which is reasonable, but it fails to consider the tendencies of those talented enough to play the game: they want admiration. They have an aesthetic generosity and, even if they have a political and material selfishness, they remain unsatisfied unless someone else can appreciate the maneuvers by which they accomplished their ends. The best audience, the audience most likely to appreciate the magnitude of the victory and the subtlety of the means, is the victims.

In any event, I told them what I told them, and I left them, making my way as expeditiously as I could to the residence of the Capelletti, where I presented myself and sought an interview with the young lady.

"She is not receiving today," Capelletto told me. He was trying to sound official and abstract, and he missed, as usual. It sounded to me as if he were describing a medium whose receptivity was impaired by sun-spots.

"I understand," I told him. "I have heard about your trouble. I realize how upsetting this must be for you. Indeed, it was my hope to be of help. If I could talk with the girl, I would try to elicit from her some signs of that filial affection and obedience that sometimes are obscured by passing events and momentary stress." There was a good deal more of this kind of thing, none of it worth remembering, let alone transcribing. I should expect that there is a fortune to be made someday by someone unscrupulous enough to put on religious garb and tell people exactly what they want to hear — that they are wonderful, fine, deserving, beautiful souls, that their guilts are baseless and groundless, their setbacks temporary, their rewards inevitable, their hearts true, and their souls saved. Anyone narcissistic enough to believe all that is probably damned anyway and only deserves to be gulled.

I was an intellectual bully, a theological thug. I got by Capelletto, who opened the door for me and thanked me for taking the time and trouble to come.

Alone with Giulietta, I asked her what she had been doing.

"Nothing," she said, her eyes big and sad, like those of a mournful spaniel.

"But you wanted to."

"Yes, but I was fighting it."

"But you were losing, weren't you."

"Yes," she admitted, looking bereft and beautiful. It was heroic of me not to run to her, embrace her, smooth the furrows of her brow with little bird-kisses. What a delicate, gorgeous, delectable creature.

"I really was trying, Fra Lorenzo, but it was so difficult. I mean, he saved my life. I owed him so much. And he came to my balcony, and. . . "

"And why weren't you thinking of the saints? Why weren't you thinking about the Holy Virgin?"

"I was," she said. "I kept saying, virgin, virgin, virgin, but that made me think of my virginity, and that made me think about Romeo."

"Why weren't you thinking about me?"

"I was thinking about you. But that was the whole point, wasn't it? That it was impossible with you. And then I thought how possible Romeo was. Not only possible, but probable. Easy! And I knew I shouldn't, but then I thought how much I wanted it and how much more he must want it, because he's a man and you've always said it was worse for men."

"Yes, it is worse."

"And if it was worse for him, and if I owed him my whole life, then didn't that include my body? And I thought about my body, and his body, and . . . oh, it was awful. I was lost, really lost. Except that the bells started to ring and the dogs were barking and there were people shouting. He ran away. And Daddy locked me up."

"You could think of me again."

"I tried that. But it just isn't the same," she said.

"That's hardly flattering."

"Fra Lorenzo! What are you saying?"

"That you could think of turning to me for help."

"You'd help me?"

"Of course."

"But this is sinful."

"No, it isn't. As St. Paul once said, it is better to marry than to burn. I can help you get out of here. And marry you, as well."

"Wonderful."

"Yes, it is."

"How will you get Daddy to agree?"

"I won't."

"Then how will you get me out of here?"

"With this." I explained to her about the green liquid, where it came from and what it did.

"So I'll go to sleep here and I'll wake up there?"

"That's right."

"It's just like a fairy tale."

"Exactly."

"I don't know how to thank you."

"Sooner or later, something will occur to you, I'm sure."

"It smells awful, though."

"Yes, it does. It's very powerful."

She had taken the phial and was sniffing it, getting herself accustomed to it, working up her nerve or balancing its admittedly disagreeable qualities with its desirable effects, thinking no doubt of Romeo. That, at any rate, was what I assumed. But then she lifted it to her lips. Fortunately, she paused to say, "Well, here goes," so that I could stay her hand.

"No, no! Not while I'm here. It would be very awkward to explain. If I came in while you were alive and left with you seeming to be dead, people might leap to all sorts of unwarranted conclusions."

"Yes, I see that. I'm sorry. But the longer I think about it, the harder it will be."

"And the nobler," I told her.

"You're sure that this is all right?"

"Of course I'm sure."

"It smells perfectly dreadful."

"Don't think about it. Think about . . . think about fornication."

"I do, all the time."

"And think of love."

"Is there a difference?"

Oh, the candor, the innocence, the purity of that child! Protected as she had been, she was utterly unsullied by the sentimental ideas of the poets and painters, and instead displayed the ingenuous directness of a small cuddly animal or brightly plumed bird. She combined the simplicity of paganism with the sweetness of Christianity and was, therefore, a model of what the Renaissance ought to have been but wasn't.

But I get carried away. I gathered the skirts of my soutane about me, and made the sign of the cross over her — just in case I'd got the proportions wrong and the potion turned out to be stronger than I'd wanted. I stopped on my way out of the house to assure Capelletto that I had warned her of the perils of disobedience and had pointed out the error of her ways. "She seemed stricken by remorse," I told him, "truly mortified and repentant. I am hopeful that within the coming days and weeks, I shall be able to build upon that feeling of chagrin and help her to correct her conduct and be the kind of daughter you deserve."

It was not difficult. The only difficult part was not to smile, not to betray my satisfaction with the beautiful neatness of how my remarks — which he was altogether happy to hear — were the preparation for the next step. I knew that he would in a short time discover his daughter's inert body. I knew that it would appear to be a suicide. And my words would then resound in his ears like a peal of huge, thunderous bells.

*   *   *

I hastened back to the church, where Romeo was hidden away in the rectory. Rosaline had made herself scarce. I composed myself, waited for Capelletto and, presto-change-o, hocus-pocus, there he was. Weeping. Wailing. Disarranging his hair, although not actually pulling it out.

There was every possible advantage on my side. He was beside himself, utterly distraught. But I knew that there would be opportunities for more careful consideration later on. I did not want him going back to the weak spot in the web I had so carefully woven. There was that terrible coincidence to which I had alluded when speaking with Giulietta. I'd had her wait until I was out of the house, but the fact remained that I'd arrived to a Giulietta who had been alive and well, and almost immediately after my departure Giulietta appeared to have died. Might not Capelletto, sooner or later, start to tug at that innocuous little thread, and might not my entire garment then unravel?

The solution was to be bold, aggressive, positively daring. My assumption had to be that the girl committed suicide. If I didn't kill her, then the next likely suspect was the girl, herself. It was a matter of some delicacy, but diffidence would not serve. As when one removes a deep splinter, the kindest thing is to cut deep and fast.

"A terrible thing," I agreed.

"I can hardly believe it," he told me.

"Neither can I. How did it happen?"

"That's the worst part of it. We don't know."

"She was depressed. Guilty. Remorseful. Could she have killed herself?"

"Of course not. Capelletti do not commit suicide."

"As a general rule, of course not."

"It would be . . . disgraceful," he said.

"Worse than that, it would be sinful," I told him.

"Impossible," he said, but he had by this time begun to

see my drift. "With religious guidance from a man like your-self, how could she even have thought of suicide?"

"Oh, no you don't. You can't blame it on me. Religious instruction cannot overcome the influence of an improper home life."

"Improper home life? Where do you get that?"

"You forget, sir, that I was your daughter's confessor. I am also the one who must decide whether Giulietta is to be buried in consecrated ground. I assume that you are here to make the funeral arrangements? I must be convinced."

"That's extortion!"

Better than extortion, it was cheek! It was a way of diverting his suspicion. Besides, I was not trying to enrich myself; the worst charge that could have been appropriately leveled was simony, I should think — but even there, my defense would have been that the girl wasn't dead, that I was not offering an inappropriate burial, that I was doing noth-ing more than many a fund-raiser has done, playing upon the emotions of a prospective donor.

"I suggested that I must be convinced," I told him, "but there are other avenues open to you. You could appeal for a verdict from Rome. Or you could apply to Cardinal Schiavone in Venice, who, if he is not occupied with his blocks and colored pencils, might devote himself to the subtleties of your situation."

"Schiavone?" Capelletto asked, and he shook his head, acknowledging the futility of seeking help from that quarter. "He's dead. Measles, I think."

"No!"

I could not think about it, not then. I was too far committed. I shook it off with barely a tremor of my left eyelid and continued in my efforts to shake down Il Signor

Capelletto and take him for as much as I could. "Sad news, indeed," I said about the late little cardinal, "but it's sad for you, too. It narrows your options even further. If the cardinal is dead, the only appeal is to the Holy Father, and that takes so long. And in the summertime, it's. . . "

I searched for the right word. "Inconvenient" is what I may have settled on, but the upward inflection suggested that it was inadequate to describe the stench a body can make in the hot months of the year, even after a relatively short time.

I watched the realization of what I was implying open like one of those paper flowers you drop into water. I had him by the baldacchinos.

"You realize," I said, "how much more difficult this news makes things for me. The decision is now wholly mine."

"That makes it worse for you?"

"Oh, yes. Think of the responsibility. Do you realize what it would mean if she had committed suicide and I were to admit her to consecrated ground?"

"What?" he asked, having a fairly clear idea of what was coming.

"My soul would be cast into infernal damnation."

He didn't say anything.

"My soul happens to have a great sentimental value," I nudged. It was wrong of me. Pushy. But impossible to resist.

"This comes at a bad time. It hasn't been a good year," he began. We were off and bargaining. We settled on a new campanile, nothing so grand as the one in Florence, but an improvement on what we'd had, which was virtually a schoolbell in a privy. That kind of donation, we agreed, would be sufficient for me to risk hell-fire.

I extended my condolences. He thanked me for my understanding and my flexibility. He took his leave.

Within an hour, the hearse arrived. In it, there was the coffin. In the coffin, there was my darling, cool to the touch, still to the most minute inspection, but alive.

I prayed that she'd make it.

*   *   *

We had to switch caskets.

We carried Giulietta down to the crypt, which was easy enough. Carrying Guilietta's nurse back upstairs was more arduous. And unpleasant. She'd begun to go a little gamey. But we managed it, Romeo and I. Rosaline held the lantern for us.

A difficult night. We had a light supper, played cards for a while, drank a fiasco of the local Soave, and went to bed early. I was nervous about Giulietta's progress, a little uneasy about Romeo, and furious with Rosaline for having dragged me into this in the first place. Thinking about the biretta didn't help either.

It now seemed to mock me, that trick of timing, that hesitation of just a beat or two. If only he'd lived another week longer, or a few days less, my path would have been clear. I'd have gone ahead, wholeheartedly. As it was, I had to watch my fondest hopes withering. There was good prospect for my short-term success — for a month or two, or even a little more if I was lucky. But I could not expect to continue to get away with it forever. Sooner or later, a priest living in a small town with a thirteen-year-old girl who is supposed to be dead . . . runs into the likelihood of having his deception exposed. And at that point, people are more apt than not to be vexed with him.

It took me many hours and many glasses of brandy

before I was able to sleep. And my dreams were awful, incoherent but always menacing, one catastrophe blurring away into another, so that I woke in the morning as stiff as if I had been beaten with clubs by all my enemies — an increasingly impressive constituency.

The stiffness wasn't all. I was positively ill, hung over, my head aching, my stomach uncertain, my mouth flannel, my nerves hot wires. Hangovers are occasions for moralists to enjoy themselves, making light of the suffering of their fellow men, quick to reiterate what the victim's own chagrin has already made clear. I'd drunk too much. And I had a funeral to do. It was a responsibility I took seriously. I have always prided myself upon my ecclesiastical performances. My elegant, somewhat nasal plainsong was torture.

I drank several tumblers of well water, to no real advantage. I considered a temporary suicide — drinking some of the potion myself. But no, that was a ridiculous idea. And so I robed myself for the requiem mass, put my best chasuble over my alb, and made my entrance.

It was a good crowd. There were all the Capelletti and their clients, dependents, and friends. There were the Montecchi, who had to come because it would have been an insult for them to stay away. There were the other dignitaries and officials of the town. The Prince was there. And the common people had come to gawk at the notables, to be fed afterwards by the Capelletto kitchens, and to get drunk, steal, and frolic as if it were a holiday.

For that poor old nurse of Giulietta's, it was a wonderful send-off, far better than she could have expected.

For me, it was torture. Only after I was well into the service, having subdued my diverse aches and frailties, was I able to perceive that the attitude of the congregation was a bit odd. There was a buzzing, a quality of inquiry and communication that resembled the chatter of little girls in a catechism class. There were glares, looks, murmurs, erratic sibilations, and all the indications of animated inattention. It was a distraction, and I looked down to see that my chasuble was not awry. What was I doing wrong? What had I failed to do?

Not until after the service, out in the graveyard, did I have a chance to make inquiries. And the trouble was that Romeo was absent.

I simply hadn't thought of it. But obviously he should have been at the funeral. Just as obviously, I couldn't have him at the funeral because he wasn't trustworthy. He knew too much. A dilemma — but I hadn't even tried to think it through. I'd kept him out of sight as a matter of cautionary instinct, and I'd been wrong. But one can be brilliantly wrong, can err in such a way as to allow for improvisation that is actually an improvement on one's original conception. It was out in the cemetery that the subdued animosities, questions, accusations, and resentments flared up, the restraints of the church architecture having given way to the loftier vaulting of heaven itself.

In loud stage-whispers, Capelletto and Monteccho assailed one another, the point of departure being, so far as I could tell, Capelletto's question: "Where is that asshole son of yours?"

"Hiding from your thugs, I think."

"Feeling guilty, eh?"

"Why should he feel guilty? He didn't kill himself."

"Maybe he should give that one more thought."

"Shshsh!" (This from the Prince.)

There may have been twenty seconds of silence before Capelletto accused Monteccho: "It's all your fault."

"Why my fault?"

"Romeo couldn't have figured this out for himself?"

"He loved her."

"Bullshit! He didn't love anyone. He was leading her on. Trifling with her."

"Bullshit!"

"Shshsh!" (Again, *il principe.*)

This time, the silence could not have lasted for ten seconds before Capelletto asked, "Why didn't he run away with her? She'd at least be alive."

"He would have, if you hadn't called out your dogs."

"He's a damned coward."

"You're crazy."

"Then why isn't he here? Criminals are supposed to return to the scene of the crime, aren't they?"

"But he didn't do it here."

"But he did it!"

"No, he didn't."

"I'll kill him!"

"Maybe that's why he's not here," Monteccho suggested, rather sensibly, I thought.

"Shshsh!" He was sounding more and more like a principal and less and less like a prince. But by this time, the coffin had been lowered into the grave, and it was time for the ceremonial shovelfuls of earth to be dumped upon it.

Now, I hadn't planned any of this. I hadn't even made allowances for the possibility that there would be this kind of animosity at the obsequies. And I certainly hadn't any way of knowing that Romeo would overhear most of this, having found a safe gargoyle behind which he could crouch, up on the corner of the transept, overlooking the burial ground.

The result was that after the departure of the mourners and their guests, both friendly and inimical, I had to confront a craven youth in the throes of terminal panic.

"They're out for my blood!" he said. "They're furious. They're really after me."

"That's not surprising, is it?"

"It's not comforting, either. I'll never get out of Verona. Someone will see me. And even if I manage to get away, there'll be no place to hide. Where can I go?"

"Norway?"

"Not far enough."

"China?" Or was Marco Polo's mantle a bit large for this moral dwarf?

"Not even there. I'm scared," he said, as if I had not managed to abstract this from his copious data.

"Well, there is a possible solution . . ."

"And that is?" The struggle between fear and distrust was written on his face in letters large enough for a child's primer.

"I have some of the potion left," I told him.

"For me?"

"Why not? You'd appear to be dead. There'd be another funeral. Both of you would be thought to have died. They'd stop looking for you. You'd be safe."

"I don't know.

"What's the matter with it?"

"I think it's dangerous."

"What courage. What gallantry. Giulietta didn't hesitate."

"Yeah, but . . . but she hasn't revived yet either, has she?"

"I was just going to have a look."

"Well, if it worked for her, I guess I could try it."

"How noble of you."

"But wait a minute," he asked. "What do you get out of all this?"

"I get the credit for having established peace in the city. My daughter may get the hand of the Prince. I've already taken Capelletto for a new campanile."

"You have? How?"

I told him that I'd expressed doubts about the possibility of Giulietta's having forfeited her right to a Christian burial. It took him a moment to figure out that meant suicide. And that, since she wasn't dead, it was funny. The wheels turned and the cogs meshed, and then the face lit up with a kind of grin.

"I'm pleased that you're pleased," I told him.

I led the way down to the crypt, where Giulietta reposed in the plain pine coffin that had been supplied for her old nurse. She seemed waxen, unmoving, inanimate. I put my ear to her chest and listened. Nothing. Or was there a faint, barely perceptible sound, a heartbeat? Or was that my own heartbeat, the pulse in my own eardrum? "I don't know," I said.

"It doesn't look good."

"Oh, no. On the contrary. It looks fine. It's supposed to look as if she's dead. The question is whether what it looks like is what it is."

"Hunh?"

"I'm not sure, but she may have a heartbeat," I said. Idly, I touched her face with my fingertips, both to soothe her and to reassure myself. Was there some sign of heat? But at my touch, either coincidentally or in response, there was a slight motion of the head, the way someone who is asleep may move, just a little, if touched. "Did you see that? Did you? She moved! She's alive!"

"No, you did that."

"I?"

"You pushed her with your finger."

"Why would I do that?"

"To make me think she's alive. So I'd take your damned potion."

It was a false accusation. But it would have been a good idea. "What a stupid idea!" I told him. I didn't want him to get a swelled head.

"Is it?"

"We'll wait. You'll see. In a few minutes, she'll come around. And you'll apologize to me — I hope."

"I hope so too."

So we sat down to wait, looking at each other, looking at her, looking at the stone floor. It was an awkward time. I suppose Giulietta would have enjoyed it if she had been conscious — her two lovers, each of them hoping that she'd wake up, breathe, stir, and each of them more than half hoping the other one dead, and yet needing the other at least for a little while longer, and therefore restrained.

It must have taken the better part of an hour before there was a discernible movement of the head and arm. And then a groan.

"See?" I said.

"I guess so."

"I feel awful" were Giulietta's first words.

"Here, have a sip of white wine. It will settle your stomach," I said.

"Oh, no. No, I can't. I think I'm going to vomit."

I think it's the mandragora. One day, someone will get the wrinkles out of it, and that potion will be a gold mine.

"My teeth feel as if they were made out of metal. And my tongue feels like a dishrag."

"Hold on," I said. "I'll get a receptacle." I hurried upstairs. I was nervous, couldn't think of what to take to her. A chalice was too small. And not quite apropos. I found a ewer. And a mop.

By the time I returned to the crypt, the mop was the more relevant instrument. I handed it to Romeo, letting him tidy up while I gave Giulietta a sip or two of wine. "It will settle your stomach."

"I feel so groggy. And my head aches."

"You'll sleep a little more. And then you'll feel fine." Actually, it takes a couple of days before one feels quite right again, but I didn't want to put Romeo off.

"Giulietta, I'm here," he said.

"Romeo? Oh, Romeo. Hi."

"A little more wine?"

She took another sip and then cuddled back down into the plush of the coffin.

"Satisfied?" I asked him.

"I guess so," he said.

"Good," I told him.

"And I apologize."

"I forgive you," I said. It was his extreme unction.

VII

WE LEFT OUR BELOVED CONVALESCENT in the crypt, and I led the way to the sacristy, where I had secreted the phials, flasks, beakers, retorts, alembics, and decanters in a cabinet holding some of our uglier reliquaries, with their grisly remains — the earlobe of St. Eusebius, for example. There was still some of the potion in my phial, but to it I had added, in a spirit of generous catholicity, a variety of deadly poisons. This was my way of having the girl to myself, getting rid of this dolt, and keeping Rosaline more or less satisfied — or at least harmless.

"Here it is," I said, holding it aloft with an eagerness and a cheerfulness that was not at all feigned.

"That? What is it?"

"Your portion of the potion."

"But what's in it?"

"You want the recipe? Oh, no. That's my little secret."

"Does it always make you throw up?" he wanted to know.

"Often," I admitted. In his case, I doubted he'd live that long. "But better sick than dead, right?"

He was not amused. He made a face that was not necessarily a comment upon the smell of the elixir. I set it down to fetch him the writing paper.

I've forgotten to mention the writing paper? The suicide note? Ah, there it goes again. It seemed to me so obvious, so abundantly clear that there would have to be a suicide note, I had assembled paper, ink, quills, a penknife, blotting sand, all the requisite paraphernalia, and had them ready on a tray. I turned away, just for a moment, so that I could turn back with the tray in my hand and say, "But first, the suicide note," and bask in his admiration that I'd thought of everything . . . but the fool had already taken the poison.

I gaped. It was an unattractive reaction, I confess, but I was nonplussed. I was minused: "No, not yet, you stupid shit!"

"Did I do something wrong?"

"Yes, you did something wrong. What do you mean by killing yourself in here? The Church is supposed to be against that kind of thing. I can't have your corpse in here. You've got to be out there, so that your body is discovered on Giulietta's grave. Isn't that tender? Isn't that sweet?"

"I'm sorry. I didn't think."

"And we need the suicide note."

"Note? What note?"

"The note that says why you've killed yourself. That's the most important part. I often think that a fair number of people kill themselves only because they've written a really good suicide note, and then they have to kill themselves because the genre requires it."

"The genre requires . . . ? I don't feel so good."

"Sit. Write."

He sat and took the quill from me. He dipped it in the ink, held it, squinted as if it were difficult to see the tip of the pen, and asked me, "What do I write?"

"Let me think," I said, alarmed by his slumping posture and the greenish cast to his complexion. "'Friends, Veronese, countrymen. . .' No, that's ridiculous. Never mind the salutation. Just write, 'It is not only grief for my beloved Giulietta.' Do you have that?" He was slumped over the paper so that the quill seemed to be protruding from the tip of his nose.

"Wake up! You can't die yet. You've got to finish the note. You've got to sign the note at least. At the bottom, you ape. Write your name R. O. M. E. Oh, for God's sake!" I had to slap him awake "M. E. O."

I could, I supposed, fill in the rest myself.

"Up! Up, you dummy! Out! Out to the graveyard!" I half pushed, half kicked, half carried him out there. That's too many halves by half, isn't it?But it took a lot of effort on my part. He was not cooperative. He staggered and kept trying to dive down onto any old grave. I arranged him on the right mound of fresh earth, left him there, and returned to do the note.

It was not an action of which I was proud. On the other hand, I'm famous for it, am I not? And it is one of the great moments in the folklore of foolish young love. For reasons that are too awful to state, the vision of the two dead lovers is one that most of mankind — and womankind — seem to envy. Dead, their love was safe from the inevitable decay that eats at those condemned to the long dwindling of matrimony.

There, I've stated it, haven't I? The dirty secret that explains the special place those two have in the shrine of Aphrodite's devotees. Any alternative, from the point of view of the quality and the intensity of the love, is less attractive. The love dies rather than the lovers. With Romeo and Giulietta, in this altogether silly version of the events, the love remains unsullied and perfect, the ideal that cannot last except in the realm of Platonic forms. The idea of the rose is eternal, but any particular rose wilts, fades, loses its petals, and dies.

And compared to Romeo, the roses have it lucky. Romeo

was out there on Giulietta's grave for . . . an hour? Two? No more than that, surely. And during that time, various villains came idly by to . . . embellish the macabre spectacle. My theory is that one of the nefarious wayfarers may have been a Capelletto dependent and, for that reason, in the hope of a reward from Signor Capelletto, he cut off one of Romeo's ears. That's more probable than that he cut off both ears, isn't it?

My guess is that the second ear was cut off by one of the Montecchi, who wanted to make the disfigurement — which would in any event be blamed on the Capelletti — look especially brutal and savage. Or perhaps he wanted the corpse to look symmetrical.

No, it has to be that he was trying to pin it on the Capelletti. The murder, I mean. Not the ear.

This is supposed to be the Renaissance, but this was positively baroque.

In any event, the moral complication is considerable. If I hadn't poisoned him, he'd have died anyway, just from having drunk the potion. Not from the loss of the ears, perhaps, but from the other attentions. It seems that he was run through several times. Even though he was probably dead by then. The assignment of responsibility becomes a matter of some intricacy.

One consequence of Romeo's death was that it became difficult (actually, impossible) for me to shake Monteccho down for the baptistery that I'd looked forward to persuading him to contribute. With Capelletto's generous pledge, it would have made a matched set.

As far as Romeo was concerned, though, I can't think that it made much difference. "When your number's up, it's up." (From the Book of Numbers?)

* * *

I was not even aware of what was going on out in the bury-patch. I was inside, attending a revival meeting. Giulietta had slept a little, but she was coming around, rapidly regaining consciousness.

"My mouth is absolutely crawly," she announced, "and my head hurts. But it was worth it. For Romeo!"

"Oh dear! Drink this."

She took a little wine, sipping with the delicacy of a cat, and then asked, "Why 'Oh, dear!'?"

I hesitated. I could have prevaricated, saying that she was dear, but I thought that it might be better to get it over with at once, insinuating the information into a mind that was not altogether alert. "Romeo is no more," I told her.

"You mean he's dead?"

"Alas, yes."

"But how? Why?"

"What difference does it make?" I asked, unaware of the complexities that, even at that moment, were being perpetrated within a hundred yards of us. "He's dead. He loved you and he's dead."

"That's sad," she said, getting the point.

"Yes, yes, it is."

"Did he despair of my coming back?"

"Oh, no. He was here, at your funeral, enjoying it all. He thought it was going to be a great joke. But he saw how angry they all were at each other, and especially at him. He thought it would be better if he did what you'd done, taking the potion so that he looked dead."

"So? So he took the potion?"

"He intended to take the potion. What he took was the

contents of the wrong flask. It was rat poison. It really did kill him."

"That's awful."

"It was a natural mistake. They were both green.

"Oh, I remember. Nasty."

I put my arms around her. "Yes," I said. "The rat poison smelled less repulsive, as a matter of fact. That may have been what confused him."

"What are you doing?" she asked.

"I'm comforting you."

"I'm quite comfortable."

"You're still woozy. You don't know what you're saying."

"Yes, I do," she said.

She was opposing my attempts to climb into the coffin with her. It was a tight fit, but intimacy knows no constraints. I'd always wondered about doing it in a coffin, ever since the days in seminary when I'd seen the most extraordinary illuminations in the work of some crude vulgarian. It is not always the best art that stays in one's head.

"Get out of here! This is my coffin!"

"It's my crypt," I reminded her. "In my church."

"I'll scream!"

"They're my walls, and they're twelve feet thick."

"You're twelve feet thick. There isn't room in here . . . "

She was quicker and more agile than I expected. Certainly, she was more agile than I. Somehow or other, I found myself in the coffin alone.

It struck me, not unreasonably, that this was an extremely peculiar and even farcical situation, the kind of thing playwrights ought to attend to and yet have not connected with Giulietta. I started to laugh. A fit of near hysteria overtook me. I could hardly get my breath. I lay back in the coffin, laughing, and she slammed the lid shut, which made me laugh all the louder. It sounded very strange, resonating in the wooden coffin and in the stone crypt. And I thought of what it would look like to some interloper, some stranger: a coffin with hysterical laughter coming out of it — and that kept me going for another several peals. It was exhaustion more than anything else that allowed me to catch my breath.

"Let me out of here!" I called out as soon as I could manage to call out at all. "Is this any way to behave to a man of the Church?"

"Is this any way for a man of the Church to behave?"

Spirit! Wit! I was charmed. I started to chuckle dangerously again, but I took deep breaths.

"But Giulietta, we've both dreamed about it."

"I never dreamed about it in a coffin'."

"Think of it as a satin-lined box bed."

"You think of it as a box bed. You're in it."

By drawing my legs up to my chest, I was able to get some purchase on the lid and push not only with my arms but my legs too. The lid popped open.

She was laughing, which was a good sign. It hadn't been anger or fright but playfulness — and I was as eager to play as she. "Ready or not, here I come."

"Stop it," she said, in mock severity. "Think of what you're doing. Think of my reputation!"

"What reputation?" I asked her. "As far as the world is concerned, you're dead. With the angels, and as safe as they from the gossips and scandalmongers."

"But this is sinful. You told me so yourself."

"If it is sinful," I said, puffing a little, for she was a fast runner, "then it is my sin. You are my victim and entirely innocent. And if that isn't enough, think how convenient it is for us that I'm a priest and can absolve you on the very instant of the commission of the sin. During every golden moment."

She stopped, feinted left, feinted right, then darted left, slipping past me like the proverbial eel.

"I think you are a very wicked man."

"Oh, yes. I admit it."

"You should fight against it."

"I did, once. I lost. It was humiliating. I find it much more graceful to give in. And more comfortable too. As you will find it, too, I'm sure."

"You're confusing me."

"Good."

She tried another of those maneuvers with the feints to one side and then the other, but I was ready for her this time. The secret was not to react too soon, not to commit myself. Like a frog on a lily pad, I just waited, and then flicked out my hand.

"Gotcha!"

"My mouth is still dry," she said.

"Have some more wine."

I let go of her to pour wine into her glass, but she did not try to escape. It was as if we had played the game and I had won. And she was the prize. These were the rules, all of them perfectly clear and mutually understood, even though no word about them had been exchanged between us. I loved her for that, aside from anything else. I loved her for everything else, too. The childish way she held the wine goblet in both hands, so that I could narrow my eyelids and see her as a young child clutching a mug, touched me deeply. The way she flicked a gorgeously delicate pink tongue across her lips when she was finished drinking aroused me enormously. She was perfection itself. I was the luckiest of men.

I reached for her again. She did not resist, but came to me, melting into my arms, letting me smell the sweetness of her body. I kissed her, and said, "I absolve you, I absolve you, and for this I absolve you. And for this. . ."

Further absolution seemed redundant.

*   *   *

Even as the time was passing, I was aware that these few hours I had managed to snatch from the jaws of eternity might be all I could reasonably expect. And the curious thing is that I was not particularly concerned. It was as if I had been transformed into one of those mayflies that is born, mates, ages, and dies in the space of a single day. It didn't matter what the length of time was, so long as the vital experiences of living were appropriately packed into the portion I had been allotted. What more can the little fly want? He has felt the warmth of the sun, smelt the air's freshness, seen — I assume — the colors of the flowers and the liveliness of the created world. He has known the vigor of youth, the tingle of lust, and the gravity of senescence before the long oblivion of death. And he is content, as I was content.

That was the day I emerged from the long tedium of my chrysalis to soar and fly in the lofty blue sky. That there was no reasonable expectation of a future — long or short — only gave a certain added sweetness to those brief moments. I was happy to have made such a bargain. She was adorable. I was wonderful. Life was incredible and fine.

Until, at length, there was a knocking at the door. There is always a knocking at the door, sooner or later. Some churl from the outside world appears to remind us that we are not only mortal and imperfect but incapable of anything more than an unsettling glimpse of bliss, that ecstasy is, by its very nature, transient, and that the unlovely envy the everyday world seems to feel for the beautiful and the extraordinary will eventually triumph.

It was Rosaline.

"Come in, my child," I told her.

"Don't you 'my child' me!" she snapped. She was unhappy at having had to wait so long at the door. I'd answered her knock as quickly as I could, but it had taken me some time to compose myself and climb the stairs.

"Don't be peevish," I told her. "What's the matter?"

She was distressed at more than the long wait at my threshold. "The whole plan was ridiculous. From the very start, it was stupid and . . . irrelevant. There isn't peace in Verona. Everybody still hates everybody else, and the Prince is depressed. He's decided that he wants to abdicate. He can't stand it anymore."

I offered her some wine, sat her down, and tried to think what to tell her. "He's not likely to abdicate, is he?"

"I have no idea," she said. "If you want to know the truth, he's thinking of applying to some religious order. He is talking about the contemplative life."

"Absurd. He doesn't have the talent for it."

"You think you do?"

"I'm not a contemplative. But that's beside the point. Why would that be so bad? If he did join the Church?"

"It has no doubt slipped your mind — or you managed years ago to put it out of your mind — that it is not usually a part of ecclesiastical etiquette for monks to marry. And if the Prince doesn't marry me, you're in deep trouble."

As if on cue, Giulietta appeared, wandering into the anteroom in which I had been sitting.

"Oh," Rosaline said, "I see. I see it all now. It suddenly becomes clear."

"I don't believe the two of you have met," I said, hoping to change the subject.

"You must be out of your mind," Rosaline said. "And I must have been out of my mind to listen to you. You weren't trying to help me at all. Or them. All along, you've wanted her for yourself. The hell with Romeo. The hell with me. The hell with Verona. Well, I say, the hell with you. And that's not all I'll say, either."

"You've said quite enough already."

"I haven't started. I'll tell the whole city about you. You killed Romeo, didn't you?"

"He killed her nurse. He had it coming. Besides, it's complicated."

"You killed Romeo?" Giulietta asked.

"Of course not."

"Just so you could get me in that coffin?" Giulietta asked. It wasn't a criticism. She was delighted that somebody had cared enough, the way her nursery stories had promised.

"A coffin?" Rosaline asked.

"I have a bad back," I explained.

"Fra Lorenzo, who is she?" Giulietta asked.

"My daughter, Rosaline," I said.

"Your what? How can you have a daughter?"

"I should have thought that would by now be perfectly clear."

"Oh, for God's sake," Rosaline said.

"Patience, patience," I admonished her. "You were, yourself, sweet and innocent once. I can't remember you that way, but I suppose you must have been."

"And I can't remember you this way," she said. "I've always thought of you as being shrewd, a little selfish perhaps, but reasonable. I just don't understand you now. You've thrown away my hopes and my future for nothing. You can't expect anything with her. It can't possibly last. It's . . . folly. It's stupid!"

"Yes, I suppose it was," I had to agree.

"What were you thinking of?"

"I wasn't," I said, truthfully. "I am not the rationalist you've accused me of being. I was hardly even rational. I just supposed — as men of faith do — that if I followed my instincts, things would work out. I let myself be carried by the tide of events."

"You? A man of faith? Don't make me laugh!"

"I'm not attempting to be amusing. I'm telling you the truth. I wasn't claiming to be a man of faith; it was only a comparison. I don't know how to explain it any better."

"But what has happened is that you've ruined yourself. And her. And me, of course."

"I'm sorry about her and about you. But as for myself, I don't seem to mind much. I was . . . and still am . . . quite prepared to follow those instincts to the brink of catastrophe and beyond."

"A tragic figure? Is that what you're claiming to be now? The overweening pride, I can see, but the rest of it isn't exactly a fit."

"No, it isn't."

"I have no idea what either of you is talking about," Giulietta said, annoying me a little, I must confess. This wasn't Rosaline's fault and I couldn't properly blame her, but she was the occasion for my discovery — inevitable, but still a discovery — that Giulietta wasn't perfect.

"We are talking about you, my dear," I told her.

"Oh, good."

"Good? What's good?" Rosaline said, picking up on Giulietta's comment as if to demonstrate that the girl was as empty-headed as . . . as she seemed to be. "It is an absolute disgrace. A disaster. It couldn't *be* any worse."

"I suppose it could," I said.

"Oh? How?" Rosaline asked.

I hadn't meant anything in particular. It was one of those generalized remarks, but as I tried to apply it, imagining that she might tell the Prince, that she might tell Capelletto or Monteccho, that she might threaten to tell . . . "That's it!" I said, like Archimedes in the tub. "I've found it. I see!"

"You see? What do you see?" asked Giulietta, who thought that this was all very dramatic and exciting.

"I'm not sure I want to know," Rosaline said.

"I'm not sure that I can tell you," I said. "It isn't a plan, doesn't have conditions and results, isn't strictly logical. It is a vision, a kind of serene understanding and confidence . . ."

"You're missing beads on your rosary. You are absolutely beyond hope."

"Exactly! But trust me. You have, at this point, no choice anyway."

"How wonderful!" Giulietta said.

I was so transported by the loftiness of my vision that I made no sarcastic remark of any kind. I remember resisting the pun that occurred to me about how children should be obscene but not heard . . .

I expect it was just as well.

VIII

THE PALACE WAS AGGRESSIVELY UNIMPRESSIVE. What the Prince hoped to do, Rosaline had often assured me, was to set an example for the burgeoning middle class — the Montecchi and the Capelletti mostly — of restraint and good taste. Instead of passing harsh sumptuary laws that would make him feel like a tyrant but have no other effect, he hoped to use his influence, his position, the authority of his lineage, and the drabness of his clothing and furnishing to show how silly, useless, and meaningless were the lavish displays of the bourgeoisie. But it didn't work. Instead, he was an object of their contempt. They threw their extravagant dinner parties, made their ostentatious donations to the poor and to the Church, and staged elaborate ceremonies on any pretext, because they could afford to. And they assumed that if the Prince did not do such things, it was because he couldn't. Ergo, he was of no account, of no consequence. The only gravitas they understood was of the purse.

The Prince, having struck this somewhat awkward pose of asceticism, made the best of a bad beginning by attempting to brazen it out and earn a reputation as an eccentric — which was about right, I think. He was an eccentric. (On the other hand, I don't think I could have named a dozen centrics in all Italy.)

His trouble was that he had taken his education too seriously. He had been taught, as many princes are, that their office is not so much an opportunity for the exercise of power as it is a responsibility, an obligation. He had been drilled with that nonsense until he believed it, or took it for such a commonplace as to be unable to challenge it — which is, as the Church has demonstrated, exactly the same thing. Maybe it's even better. There are crises of belief, but there are seldom crises of incuriosity or dullness.

At any rate, he took very seriously his duties toward his *popolo*. Which is what he called them with a heartiness that was almost democratic. The *popolo*, as if they were all posing for genre paintings around tables of regional food, ready to play their antique instruments and do peculiar dances that would display their curious costumes and handicrafts. Rosaline put up with this earnestness a lot better than I could, but then she hoped to be princess someday. And concerned about losing that hope, her expression wavered between fury and dismay, while I, who could look forward to nothing better than excommunication, an auto da fé, and burial in a ditch along some highway, was poised and cheerful.

The Prince was more or less comatose. He had been drinking a good deal. And he wasn't used to it. It's always the amateur drunk you have to watch out for. It took some doing, but she managed to rouse him.

"It's all my fault," he said, which was an impressively stupid remark, even for him.

"Rubbish," I said, in a friendly tone.

"If only I had locked up Romeo yesterday. If only I'd been able to catch him. We all knew why Giulietta killed herself. I could have locked him up — and protected him. No man is an island, and when any man's promontory gets cut off. Oh, it's just too sad!"

"Get hold of yourself," Rosaline counseled.

"It wasn't your fault," I said. "It wasn't murder, anyway. It was suicide."

"What?" Rosaline asked.

"Suicide," the Prince told her. And then he realized what he'd said, turned to me, and asked, "Suicide?"

"It was grief over Giulietta's death that drove him to it," I said, thinking about the note I now wished I'd made time to write.

"That would be so sad and so noble," the Prince said, his eyes half closed so that he could imagine it. "That would set us all an example, wouldn't it? Except that it's impossible."

"Why?" I asked

"I saw the body," he told me.

"So?"

"What kind of fool do you take me for?" he asked. (In Latin it could serve as his motto, emblazoned on his crest.) "Do you mean that he cut off his ears and then killed himself, running himself through with his sword many times, and then putting his sword back into its scabbard?"

"No, of course not," I conceded.

"Aha! Or that he killed himself and then cut off his ears?"

"Yes."

"What?" Rosaline asked.

"Only he didn't do it himself," I explained.

"He didn't kill himself, himself?" the Prince asked, his brow furrowed a little

"He didn't cut off his ears himself, himself. He took poison, went out to Giulietta's grave, and lay down upon it to bid farewell to her and to life itself. Then various thugs, knaves, rogues, and low-lifes showed up to cut off ears, other parts of the body for all I know, and run him through. But it was a suicide. He died for Giulietta. And to save us."

"He died to save us?" the Prince asked. "That has a familiar ring."

"He left a note. A touching declaration of his love for Giulietta and a plea for civil harmony and brotherhood. You're going to use that note. And it will shame the city into an attempt at decent behavior."

"Terrific," Rosaline said with a sarcasm the Prince didn't pick up. He was thinking of his pet project — peace.

"Where is the note?" he asked.

"I haven't written it yet," I told him.

"You what?"

"Haven't written it yet," I said, enunciating slowly and clearly so that even he could understand. "I'm working on it."

"Working on it," he said, repeating the phrase to make sure he'd got it right.

"That's right," I told him. One must reward that kind of effort.

"Not Romeo?" he asked.

"Romeo can't," I told him. "Romeo's dead."

"Oh, of course," he said. "I do have the feeling that you're being less than candid with me."

"He's lying to you," Rosaline said.

"That's putting it harshly," the Prince said, displaying his usual tact and courtesy.

"I don't think so," she said, as if I weren't standing there. "He's behaved very badly and now he's lying to you about it."

"About what?" the Prince asked. "Did Romeo commit suicide or not?" He asked the question looking at Rosaline rather than at me. I thought that it was interesting — neither threatening nor reassuring, but merely interesting, in an objective and intellectual way — to hear what she'd say. She hadn't been there, after all.

"I have no idea," she said. "That's not what he's lying about. It might even have happened as he's told you. It's too stupid for him to have made up."

"I see," the Prince said, not seeing anything.

"It's Giulietta," Rosaline said.

Ah, well. There it was.

"Giulietta is not dead."

"But we buried her!" the Prince said. This time, he looked at me, which was appropriate inasmuch as I had officiated.

"The coffin was empty," Rosaline said.

"Wrong," I said. "It wasn't empty. There was a body." I explained about the nurse, whom Romeo had killed, following the suggestion of Rosaline for the machinery of the meeting of the two.

"But that's awful," the Prince said.

"But that's not the worst of it," Rosaline said, and she told the Prince about Giulietta and me, and how I'd seduced her and corrupted her. The tone was wrong, but the events were more or less correct.

"That's incredible," the Prince said.

"The only thing I don't understand is how he got Giulietta away from the Capelletti," she said.

I explained about the potion.

"That's unspeakable," the Prince said, accurate for once.

"So?" I asked.

"So?" Rosaline asked.

"So?" the Prince asked.

"So, do we let the world know? Or do we continue as we were. I'll finish the suicide note."

"Finish? Is it started?" Rosaline asked.

"Oh, yes. It's signed, at any rate. He really did sign it," I told them.

As gently and as cheerfully as I could, so as to encourage calm and reasonableness, I explained the alternatives to the Prince. We could either tell the truth and watch the city destroy itself in an orgy of blood-letting, poisoning, and mayhem that would be, for a change, almost justifiable. Or we could tell a few lies, letting the city know how the star-crossed lovers had died because of their petty squabbles and trivial enmities. They could do as they liked. I didn't much care. I'd set it all up for them. My job was done.

"You're a villain," the Prince said, but it was only an idle reflection. I paid him no mind.

"That's absolutely brilliant," Rosaline said.

"Let me know," I said, and I turned to leave.

"Wait!" the Prince called.

"Your Highness?" I asked.

"How can we hope to keep this quiet?"

"Why not?" I asked. "Nobody knows but the three of us. And Giulietta, I suppose."

"Four people? Keep a secret? Impossible! Not in Italy!"

"Not anywhere," I said, "but if they have good reason. . ."

"I don't see it, yet."

"You'd have to marry Rosaline. That would keep *her* quiet."

"And you? And Giulietta?"

"Rosaline is my daughter," I told him. "I'd be most reluctant to do anything to embarrass her. On the other hand, if you didn't marry her, then I'd be tempted — as she would be — to make you look as bad as possible. To frustrate you. To deprive you of what you've always longed for."

"Peace in Verona," he said.

I nodded. I knew how it felt when Zeus nodded. It was wonderful. I'd won. I could make them do whatever I wanted. It was lovely, lovely, lovely.

"Let me have the note, as soon as you can," the Prince said.

"Within the hour," I promised.

"Father, thank you," Rosaline said.

"My child," I pronounced, and made an exit.

*   *   *

The ridiculous version of the passion of Romeo and Giulietta that has been performed by traveling mummers and itinerant puppeteers is a reenactment of the version we performed, Rosaline, the Prince, and I, in his audience chamber for the benefit of Monteccho and Capelletto and their wives, who deserved nothing better. Suffering does not ennoble. On the contrary, if it does anything it exaggerates the peevish and nasty tendencies that were there before. Both Monteccho and Capelletto were in particularly foul form, each having been pricked on by grief to new heights of pettiness.

Before I had a chance to say anything, and even before the Prince had a chance formally to open the meeting, they began hurling taunts, imprecations, and threats at one another. Monteccho was particularly picturesque, suggesting that he was going to dig up Giulietta's coffin.

"What on earth for?" the Prince asked.

"I want what the Bible says I have coming to me."

"The Bible? What does it say?" I asked.

"You know what it says," Monteccho told me. "I get to cut off Giulietta's ears."

"You what?" Capelletto asked, hand on sword hilt.

"Oh, yeah. Right there in the Bible. It says I got a right."

"I don't think so," I started to suggest.

But he was ready for me. "What else does it mean, then? 'An eye for an eye,' and 'A tooth for a tooth,' right? So, an ear for an ear."

"The Bible doesn't mean it that way," I said.

"That's what it means to me," Monteccho insisted.

"That's . . . Protestantism."

"Even Protestants don't go around cutting off ears," the Prince said.

"Most Protestants don't," I agreed. "But look here, Monteccho. I appreciate your distress. Still, you must try to forgive and forget. Turn the other cheek."

"I don't want the cheek. Just the ears."

"That's disgusting," the Prince said.

"That's enough," Capelletto said. "I'm going to crush you like the little cockroach you are. You're going to be nothing but a dirty stain on the bottom of my boot, you understand?"

They both had their swords out, now.

"Stop," the Prince said. "You know not what you do," he said, going Biblical on us, which turned out to be a mistake. "You have eyes and you see not, ears and you hear not. . ."

"I don't have any ears. He's got the ears," Monteccho cried. His sword was up, and of some danger not only to Capelletto but to everyone else in the room.

"Romeo killed himself," I said.

"He what?" Monteccho asked.

"He killed himself, himself," the Prince said, showing that he had been paying attention.

"I don't believe you," Monteccho said, addressing me more than the Prince.

I was able to show him the note. It was Romeo's signature. I read the body of the letter, some blather about how Giulietta died a victim of ambition and political enmity, and how he was taking his own life in protest against the system, wishing only that all factions and families, all men everywhere, regardless of race, creed, or national origins, could live together in harmony and brotherhood. Blah, blah, blah. All you need is to get the tune right, and then everything follows.

The two antagonists were chastened. They embraced. Rosaline and the Prince embraced. I took my leave as expeditiously as possible, feeling that the demands of symmetry were that I, too, should be embraced, as tenderly as possible.

*   *   *

All done?

It appeared to be. And I had a sense of disappointment. I suppose I still do. In a better ordered universe, there would have been an apotheosis, a bodily translation to an eternity in the stars. Some punctuation of some sort.

Instead, having put Verona to rights, I had nothing to look forward to but the diminution of our ecstasy, or our apprehension by the authorities, cleric or laic, through some farcical slip on my part. It couldn't last, and I didn't much want to know what the actual machinery of our undoing would be.

I confess that I had insufficient faith. If you're really good enough or bad enough, then nature takes care of you. Or God does — when he isn't busy with drunks and little children, or falling sparrows, or those other orders of life to which He pays particular attention.

I like to think it wasn't wickedness that did it for us, but some sort of recognition that there was a current, a tendency the events had in themselves, their own impulse and energy, which seems at time to suggest Divine Providence. But having made such a suggestion, I am reminded that Divine Providence could have had no more unlikely agency than that which came to my door — knock, knock — in the form of a Papal Nuncio. The Vatican itself!

Obviously, the Prince, knowing how fragile was the semblance of tranquility in his city, had turned his mind to the minimization of risks, had thought of me, had realized that I had to be got rid of and that the easiest way to do this was to have me promoted out of Verona. Or maybe it wasn't so obviously the Prince who thought of this. More likely, Rosaline was covering herself, using the Prince and, at the same time, doing me a service or what she believed to be a service.

At any rate, there he was, a fine figure of a fellow with a resonant basso voice, a distinguished mane of silvery hair, a set of natty vestments, and more of a sense of humor than one might expect of a nephew of a Pope's illegitimate daughter.

"Fra Lorenzo," he boomed, "we have business to discuss." He had, actually, a conversational boom. With him, "Please pass the salt" turned into a recitative, and "Thank you very much" became practically an aria.

"Business? With me? I am not worthy," I said.

"That's perfectly true; you aren't," he intoned. "Nevertheless, events have sorted themselves out nicely, haven't they? Where is the girl?" The last question ended on a declining fourth of such grace that I hardly knew whether to answer or applaud.

"Girl? Girl?" I gurgled.

"We know all about her. We know . . . everything. And His Holiness is pleased to summon you to Rome for elevation to the College of Cardinals."

"Me?"

He nodded. "And now, where is the girl?"

"What is to become of her?" I asked. Already I understood that it was out of my hands. I could struggle if I chose, but I knew I was hooked and could see the gaff clearly enough. If there was any question, it was whether it would be quick and clean or slow and dirty.

"A convent, I should imagine."

"I see."

"A Carmelite order, I'd think."

It figured. They are the ones who never speak.

"And if I refuse?" I asked. I didn't expect to refuse. But just to be thorough, I had to ask.

"It would surprise us. It would be a mark of great piety and modesty and humility for you to refuse the biretta. And you would go where those pious, modest, humble souls have gone before you. Africa. The tour is very long. Very few of them live to return." He flashed a gorgeous smile that was clearly threatening.

I hesitated — in order at least to appear to be hesitating.

"It's better than you deserve," he said. "What other ending did you expect, after all? You can't stay here. You must see that. Whatever you choose, I'm sure it will be right for you."

"Is that so? I'd have to give it some consideration."

"The general proposition? Or your immediate decision?"

"Both. Except that I suppose you want some answer right away."

"I'm afraid so."

"I shall miss her."

"Yes, of course," he said, "but you will have cause for relief, as well. Thirteen is a splendid age, but they get to be sixteen and seventeen and turn giggly." He said it with such world-weariness, such exquisite fatigue, such fervor, that I could only imagine he had shared the experience. My guess, now, is that it was all in the incredible voice production and that what was sympathetic was the vibration in his sinuses. Still, it was a good feeling to have the understanding of the Church.

I asked him for half an hour. He offered five minutes. Five minutes was not enough. But it was ample for a mute farewell. I tried to comfort Giulietta, tried to explain to her what I did not understand myself. We held each other and wept. And then I went away.

As the Cardinal of Venice, I have few duties. My secretary is an agent of the Council of Ten and he makes all the decisions. I am a ceremonial figure, mostly, a kind of opulent prisoner of my regalia. That perfect love that can never decay, the eternal conjunction that Romeo and Giulietta are supposed to represent . . . is ours, Giulietta's and mine.

I assume she thinks of me. In a Carmelite convent, I can't imagine what else she'd be doing.

And I think of her. As the fish thinks of water, the bird thinks of air, or the tree thinks of earth, I think of her.